THE AUTOMATIC AGE:
BACKBONE OF NIGHT

Written and Illustrated by
GMB CHOMICHUK

yellow dog

Yellow Dog
(an imprint of Great Plains Publications)
320 Rosedale Ave
Winnipeg, MB R3L 1L8
www.greatplains.mb.ca

Great Plains Publications gratefully acknowledges the financial support provided for its publishing program by the Government of Canada through the Canada Book Fund; the Canada Council for the Arts; the Province of Manitoba through the Book Publishing Tax Credit and the Book Publisher Marketing Assistance Program; and the Manitoba Arts Council.

Design & Typography by Relish New Brand Experience
Printed in Canada by Friesens

LIBRARY AND ARCHIVES CANADA CATALOGUING IN PUBLICATION

Title: Backbone of night / GMB Chomichuk.
Names: Chomichuk, G. M. B., author.
Description: Series statement: Automatic age ; 2
Identifiers: Canadiana (print) 20220142165 | Canadiana (ebook) 20220142173 | ISBN 9781773370798 (softcover) | ISBN 9781773370804 (ebook)
Classification: LCC PS8605.H652 B33 2022 | DDC jC813/.6—dc23

ENVIRONMENTAL BENEFITS STATEMENT

Great Plains Publications saved the following resources by printing the pages of this book on chlorine free paper made with 100% post-consumer waste.

TREES	WATER	ENERGY	SOLID WASTE	GREENHOUSE GASES
5	410	2	17	2,220
FULLY GROWN	GALLONS	MILLION BTUs	POUNDS	POUNDS

Environmental impact estimates were made using the Environmental Paper Network Paper Calculator 4.0. For more information visit www.papercalculator.org

Canada

FSC
www.fsc.org
MIX
Paper from responsible sources
FSC® C016245

For my mother who whispered thus:

"All experience is an arch wherethrough
gleams that untravelled world whose margin
fades for ever and for ever when I move."
—ALFRED LORD TENNYSON

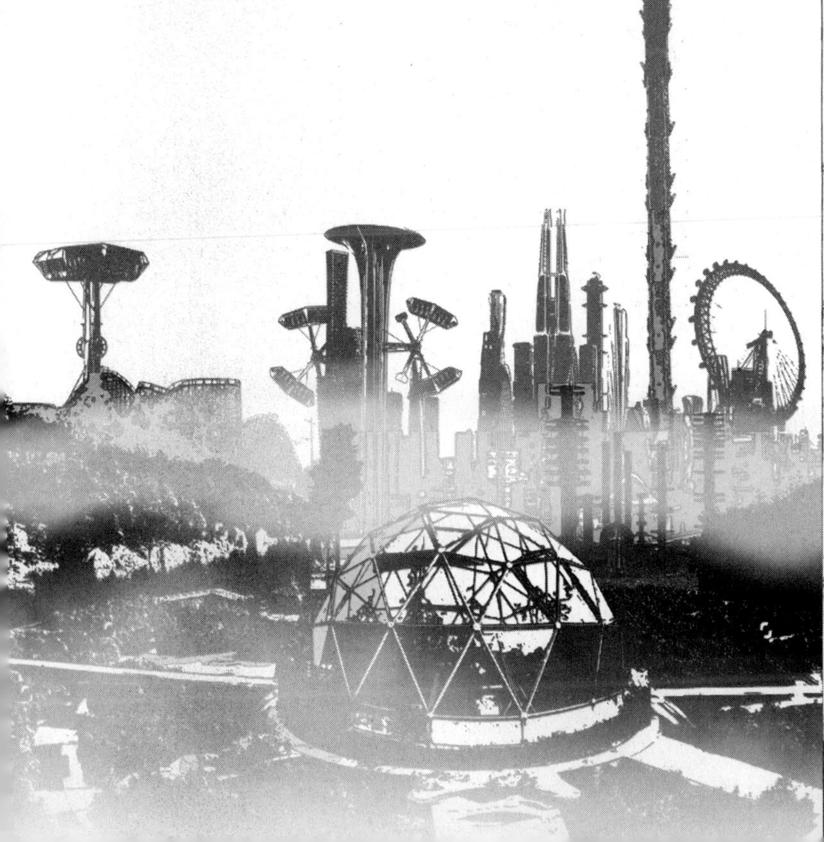

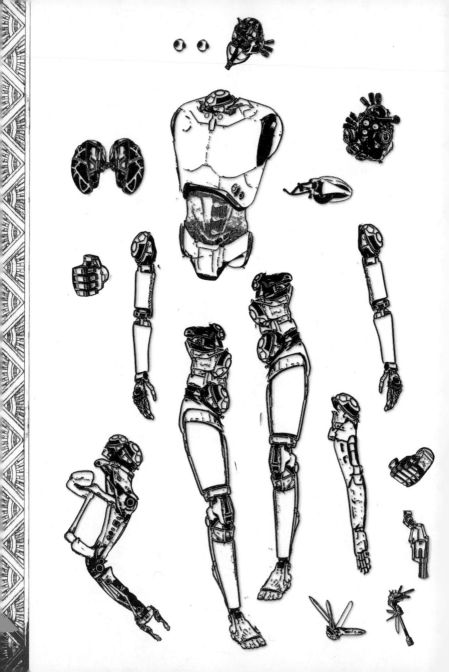

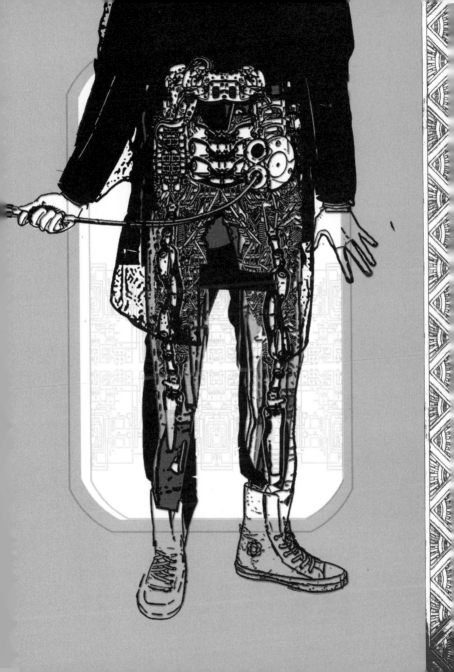

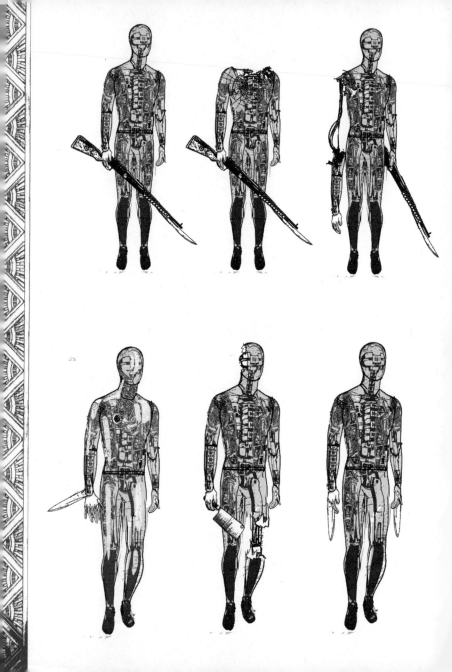

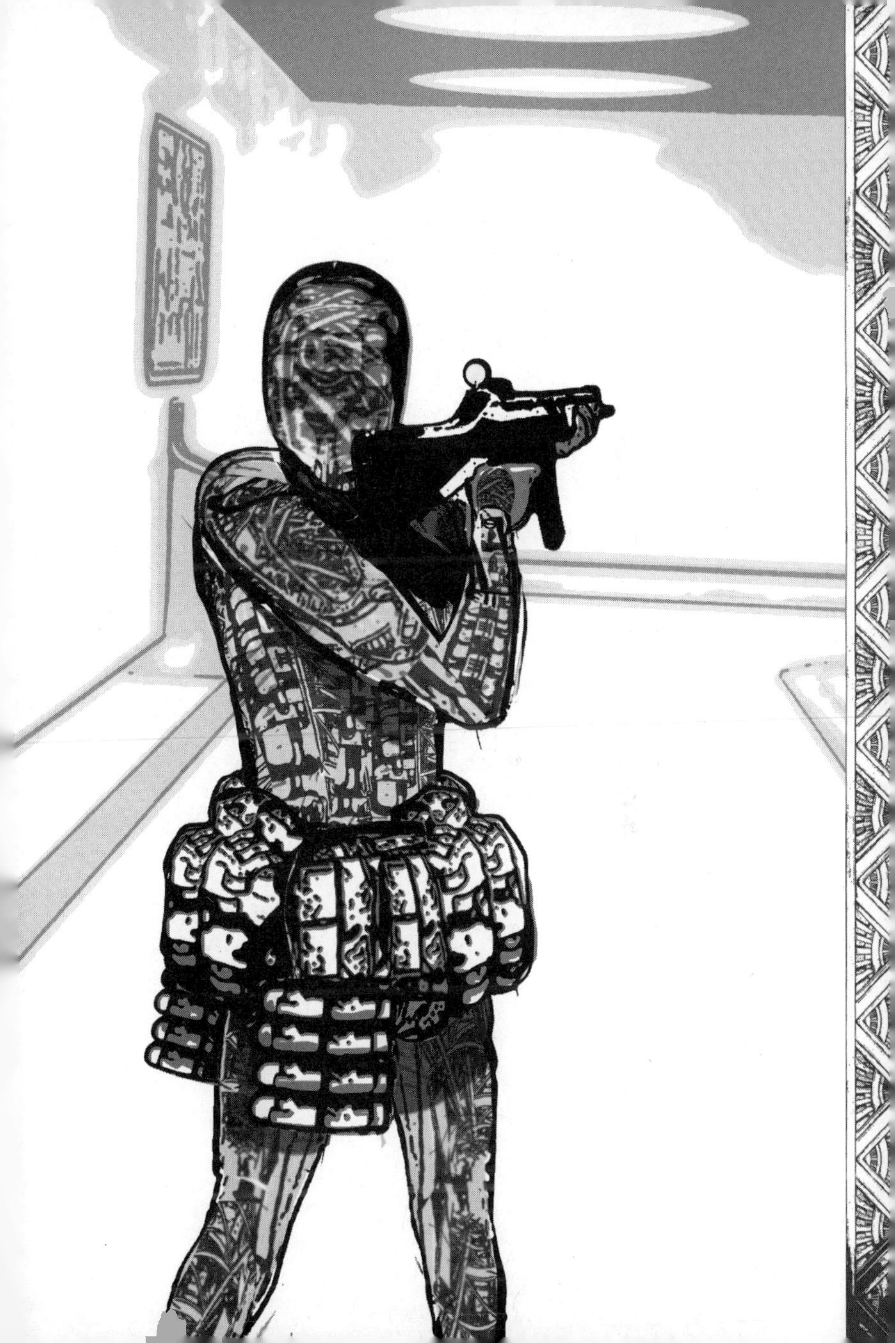

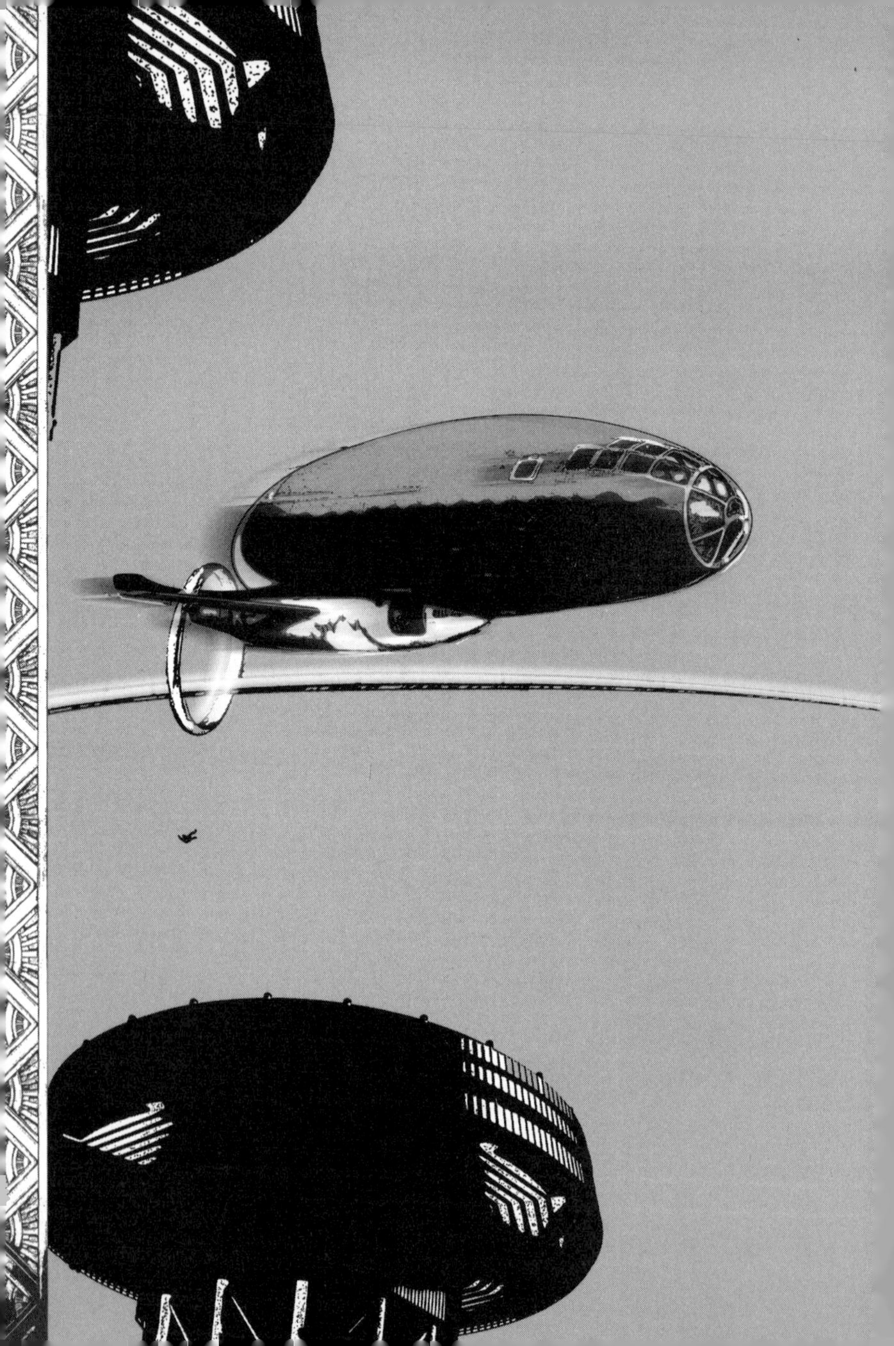

//THEBACKBONEOFNIGHT//

//MEETANDTREAT//

Barry and Kerion had come a long way.

When The Last Train had brought them to this continent, it had been daytime, so they couldn't see the space elevator. But when night had fallen, Kerion had pointed it out to his son, and Barry found himself obsessed.

The Backbone of Night was a stack of lights, false stars that went up and up in a line until you couldn't figure out where they merged with real stars. It was an elevator that went all the way into orbit. It had taken nearly a month to get close enough to see it. Of course, once they saw it, they had to go and see it up close.

"I thought it was called Funny Landing."

"It is, but the locals don't call it that. Didn't."

"Is anyone left up there?" Barry asked.

"I doubt it," Kerion said, "but maybe. *We're* still down here after all."

The fighting had clearly been worse here than where they came from. A more organized resistance, perhaps, or bigger defenses. The population here had been less surprised by the attack. Whatever their preparations, there were now perhaps only a few hundred people alive on the earth. Automatics were rebuilding everything; some parts of the city sprawls were literally crawling with repair robs. The automatic robotic society that had supported humanity kept right on doing what it had been designed to do. It cleared up the messes that people made and reset each day with a promising new deserted utopia.

So Barry and Kerion had to go slowly, had to go carefully, without alerting the auto systems that there were people to care for. The listless robots, which would automatically take care of them, were part of a network. The autovolts, it seemed, monitored that network for signs of humanity's remains. It was very hard to walk past restaurants and supermarkets and juice bars and produce stands, hydroponic bistro automats and robodegas and see all the unreachable delights within. For if they did step through the front doors of shops or restaurants and the automatics whirred and clicked and opened to greet them and to treat them as they had been designed, then somewhere not far away, an autovolt would begin its inexorable march to find them. It would follow the clues of the power they used until it found the remaining human occupants. Barry and Kerion survived by keeping on the move, taking what they needed, and trying to be long gone before an autovolt came to kill them.

To keep safe, these days Barry and Kerion hunted stray vending machines.

//SLOWANDWOOZY//

The bow thrummed and released the arrow, which struck true and solid. The vending robot walked three more shaky steps, then fell over sideways, the arrow standing upward toward the sky.

Kerion and Barry went over to it; the square cooler had opened when it fell and spilled out refrigerated sodas, sandwiches, and snack tubes into the tall grass.

"Nice shot Barry, and see? You did it *without* the autosight."

"They're slow."

"Well, help me."

The vending rob struggled to right itself, but Kerion put a boot on it, holding it down. The arms and legs swayed back and forth like those of a beetle on its back.

"I have fallen over," it said. "Please remain at a safe distance."

"I feel bad."

"We won't kill it; it'll just be a bit woozy. Before you know it a repair robot will be here to help it."

They disassembled part of the battery case and hooked up the charger. It took ten minutes to get what they needed in food, water, and power. They hoped that on whatever monitor system there was it looked like the vending machine had fallen over and was losing power.

Kerion handled a narrow bandolier of charging cells, doing a deft job of disconnecting the power relays carefully. Barry's dad needed the power packs just to keep walking. He'd lost his legs and much of his abdomen in the 7th War. The VA had provided the prosthetic automatic chassis, which needed to be taken apart regularly for maintenance and cleaning. As long as he kept eating well, the automatic inside it could keep the artificial organs going the way they should.

The battery powering the chassis lasted around six hours now. It used to be longer, but it had been faulty before the Last Christmas, and after the autovolts came— well now they had what they had and cared for it as best they could.

It was hard to imagine what would have happened if he hadn't been partially automatic when the autovots arrived at The Last Christmas.

"That'll do for a day or two if I'm careful, but we'll need to find an outlet soon," Kerion said.

They worked together to stand up the vending rob and it staggered off. They liked to let the vending robots wander away in case the repair robot reported the damages to autovolts as possible human interference. They didn't know about that exactly, but it was good to be safe. They collected what they could from the grass and went on.

They had reasoned this course of survival some time ago, on the rolling hills of a beautiful suburb. They had come to an overturned vending machine that had fallen on the grassy slope. The glass door had flipped open and it had spilled its contents. "We used to push them over when I was a kid," Kerion had said. "They fall over all the time because of how they walk, that cartoon stride." They had figured that it didn't *seem* to alert any autovolts if something "happened" in the course of a vending machine's cycle. They never knocked over the same one twice though, just to be sure. They never stayed in an area longer than a few days, just to be sure.

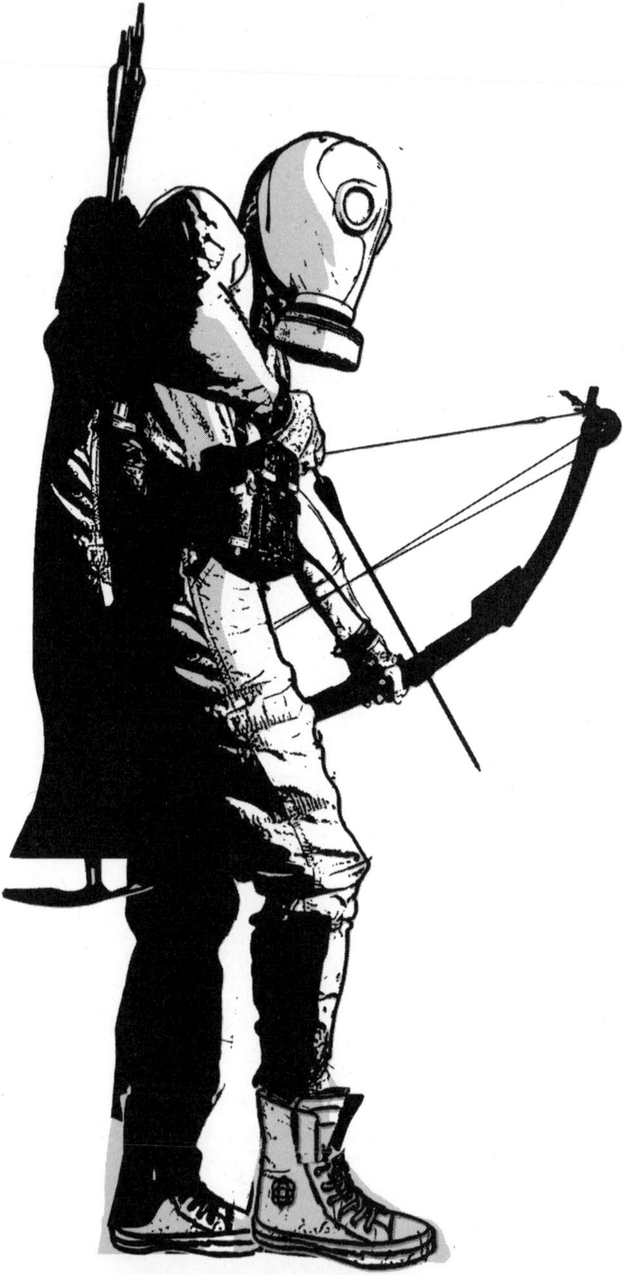

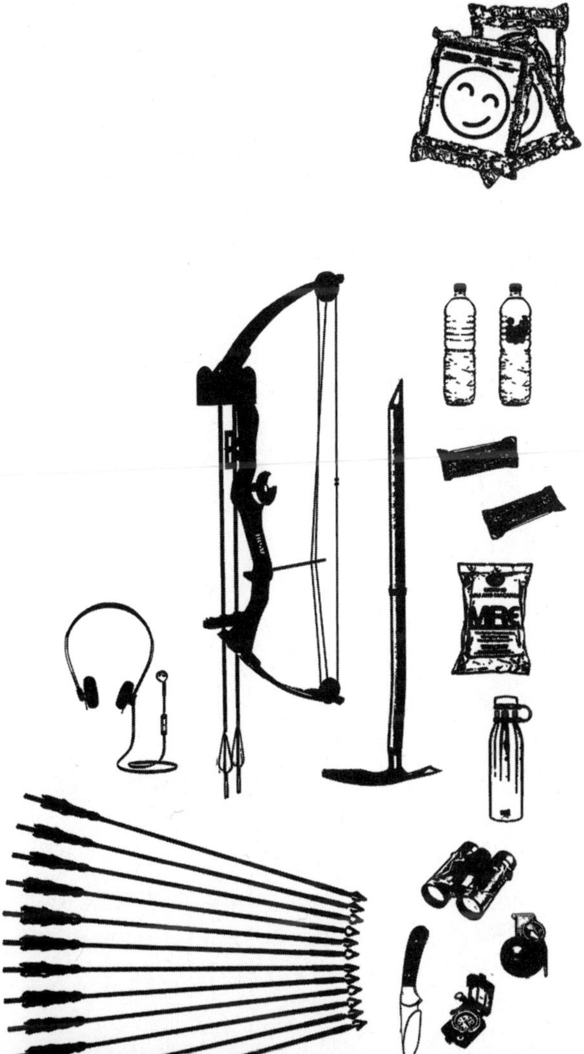
MRE

//COMPLAINERS//

They took shelter under a huge THIS WAY TO FUNNY LANDING sign at a rest stop off a belt of moving sidewalks. The sidewalks were off; the signs and lights were off too. They had come a stretch between sprawls that seemed to be without power.

Barry ran to their packs and pulled the bandolier of volters, slung it, tipped slightly sideways against the weight of the battery cells. Kerion sat, his back against the sun-warm stone as the changing sky settled in above them. The sun had just touched the horizon.

Barry extended the battery pack to his father.

"Save them." Kerion said, raising his hand.

"What? But… you need them to move."

"We can see anything on our trail from here a long way off. Let's save the volters. It takes just a minute to flat charge them if we have to move. I'll plug in, but I won't flip the switch. I'll sleep first and you keep watch. You see anything, you flip the switch and wake me."

"I don't like it."

"I know, but I don't know where we will find more volts out here. We need to conserve the ones we have for moving around."

"You can't run on a minute of charge."

"Barry. I'm afraid too. But fear and danger aren't the same thing. There is no danger, which means we need to be smart."

"What if—"

"You'll keep me safe while I sleep, then I'll charge and keep you safe. Now speaking of charge, here's yours." Kerion handed him a Vitaloaf slice.

"I don't like lemon."

"I don't like complainers." Then Kerion pulled the raygun from its holster, passed it to Barry. Made for burning out the optics of enemy satellites, rayguns had a cylinder plug for the battery shells and fired a chemical laser. They couldn't cut like the laser of the serials but burned through wood and plaster or people easily. They were built to blind satellites and worked well enough on robots.

Kerion took a spare shirt, rolled it up and placed it behind his head, and closed his eyes to sleep.

//ONLYCLOSEUP//

"Dad!"

Kerion woke, looking about for danger.

Barry hadn't switched on the volters, or had forgotten in the moment. Kerion put his thumb to the switch—

Barry was standing in front of him, a silhouette against a sky aglow in stars.

Glittering stars in the trillions, the edge of this galaxy, from within it no less.

"It's, it's so, so, is this normal?"

"We're out of the city's light pollution. That's the stars in all their glory. At this latitude, we see the galaxy more fully."

"Was this always here?"

"Yes, this is the real backbone of night."

Barry held up his hand, creating an absence of stars. Then Barry brought his thumb and forefinger together around a faraway star.

"We're so big, but only close up," Barry said.

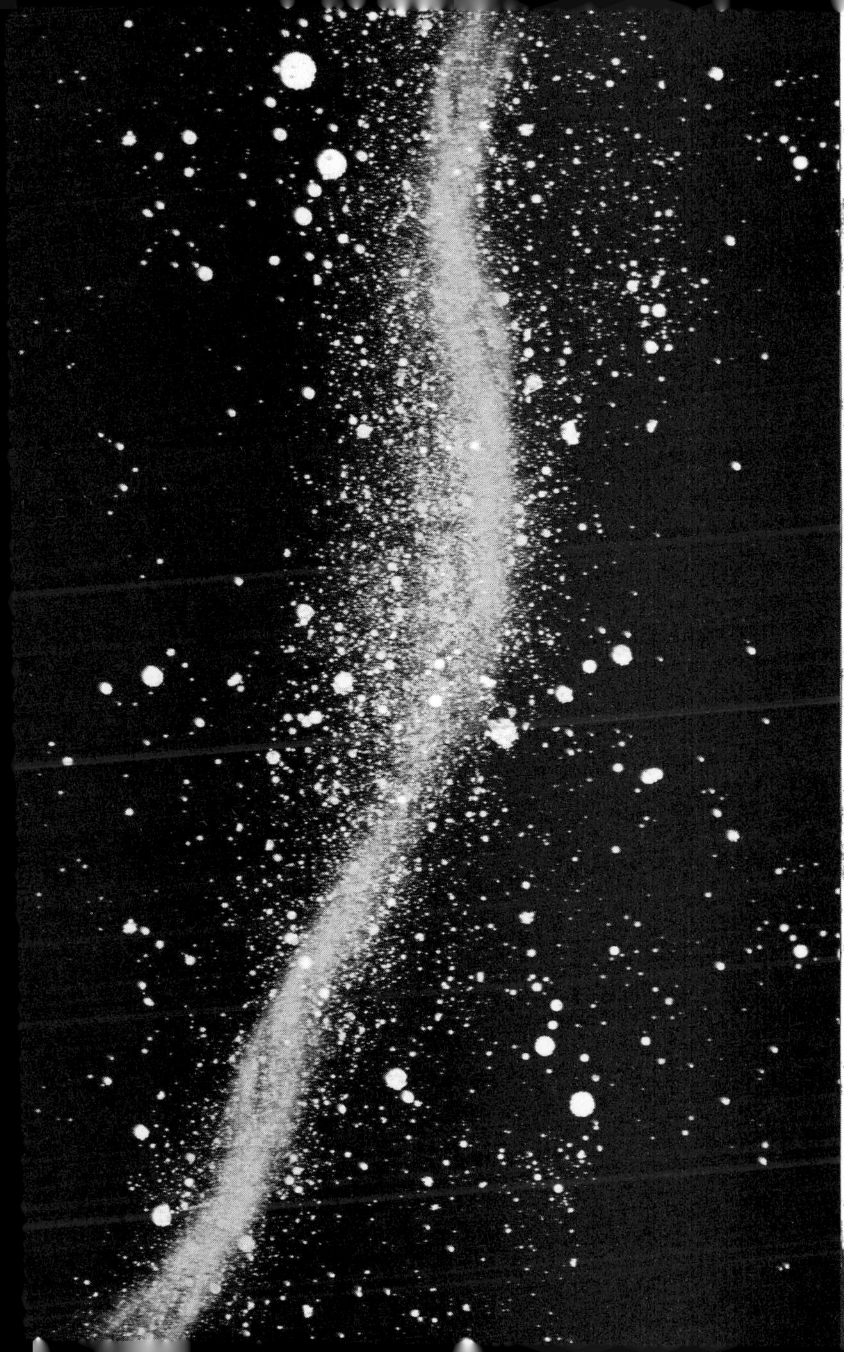

//LUCKIES//

This was the first electrical desert they had found. Kilometers without maintenance, power, or clean up. It was a dead zone between sprawls. At night they could see the lights of the Backbone and a city sprawl ahead. Behind them they could see the horizon of lights. The stars blazed overhead.

They had found a podcar line mostly blown over with dust and dirt, and they followed it. Along the way they reached a line of pods. All of the podcars were open, bubble tops up and inviting them to ride.

"Would you care to ride?" one said, startling Barry.

"If you'd like to ride, acknowledge me," the car said.

Inside Barry could see a very still, very dried, corpse.

"Dad, it saw me. I didn't think they could see."

"Must be a newer model. It's okay, we're a long way from anything. We'll be long gone before anything comes. Help me get at its battery"

"Lucky."

"How many luckies is that?"

"Eleven I think."

Keeping track of the luckies had begun a few months ago.

"What's our average?"

"Twelve or so."

Kerion sighed deeply.

"Well, that's it then. Get ready for something."

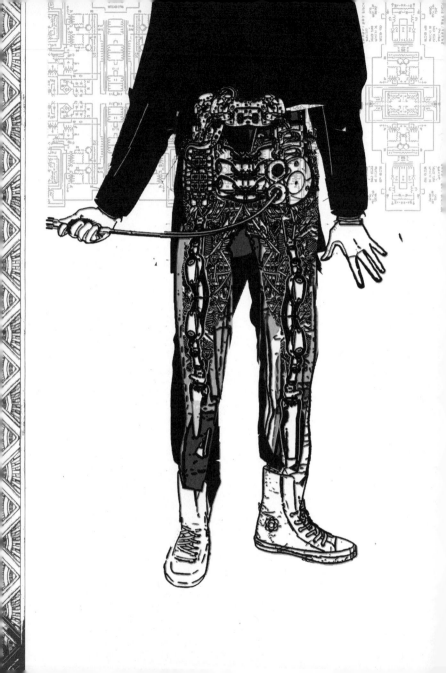

//JUSTLUCKY//

Their luck ran out at the Cheese Chunks stand, just past the Swirly Shakes, about three kilometers up the line at a Cook Cat-themed rest stop. A two-story tall cat with a chef's hat smiled at them as they approached. Its arm had been built to wave, but in the electric desert it had been stuck in the down position.

The autovolt came round the corner of the rest stop and nearly knocked into Kerion. It had one arm and damage to its face and chest but was otherwise in working order. It had a hammer in its remaining hand.

The autovolt politely declared, "I am Unit 21689865-2. Identify yourself."

"I am unit 8347-34," Kerion said.

"Incorrect, you are a human occupant."

"Exchange to verify," Kerion said.

"Exchange to verify," Unit 21689865-2 said.

Kerion lifted his jacket and shirt, took the retracted power cable by its grip, and passed it to the autovolt.

Having only one hand, it bent and placed the hammer on the ground. The autovolt then took the cable and inserted it. Kerion kept his hand on the knob under his shirt.

"Ident Verified 8347-34. You are automatic. Disconnect."

"No," Kerion said.

The autovolt reached for him, but it was not faster than the turn of the knob of Kerion's prosthetic chassis control. The autovolt jolted and sparked and fell over. A defect of Kerion's automatic chassis meant that it could surge power back through the data cable; it used up a good deal of his charge, but it killed the autovolt.

"Does that count as lucky?"

"Nope. That's preparation. All the charges I would have used up just for sleeping I used here instead."

"Then, we should have counted *that* as lucky."

"Oh, I suppose so."

//PROMISESPASTTHESKY//

That night, this close to the elevator, Barry sat staring, looking at a structure that went all the way past the sky.

It seemed so strange to him that such a structure could be there, held up by the turning of a world. His world, but right there before him was a promise of more beyond. The Backbone of Night got bigger and bigger as they got closer. At a distance it had seemed somehow more real. Now up close it seemed impossible to have achieved.

"Wow."

"It is something."

"How did they build it?"

"I have no idea."

"Magic."

"It sure seems like it."

"What's all that down there? It's so green."

Barry squinted and looked from their ridge down into the basin and the city sprawl that connected the space elevator to the earth.

"I don't know, that looks like the whole thing is an amusement park if you can believe that, some sort of green space there, and that, I guess is the community. I can see a train line, but it's mostly buried like the line we came down. Not sure why robs aren't clearing it."

"Not that. *That*," Barry pointed.

Barry gestured to the barren hills south of the community between them and the elevator. Perspective seemed to alter as he looked there.

"Look how big they are."

Kerion had seen them. Kerion had hoped Barry wouldn't notice. He had hoped he could keep his son fixated on the tower and head straight for it.

"Can we go there?"

Kerion had hoped Barry wouldn't ask. "Sure."

"You don't want to go there."

"..."

"We made a deal. If nothing is chasing us, I get to choose the path."

It was true. That *was* the deal.

"Your father keeps his promises."

//SOFLASH//

"What are these? Like Jet Jumpers only huge. They are so flash."

Kerion didn't exactly know what they were, but he was familiar with the type of thing that they were.

"What's flash?"

"Something kids say at school—said at school. It means interesting, exciting, new."

"Heavy shells of some kind."

"Like you flew in the war?"

"These are very different. Bigger obviously, but that shape, not sure what it's for. I don't know what they were supposed to do. But whatever it was, it didn't work."

"It looks like a valley of sleeping giants."

"Let's be careful not to wake them."

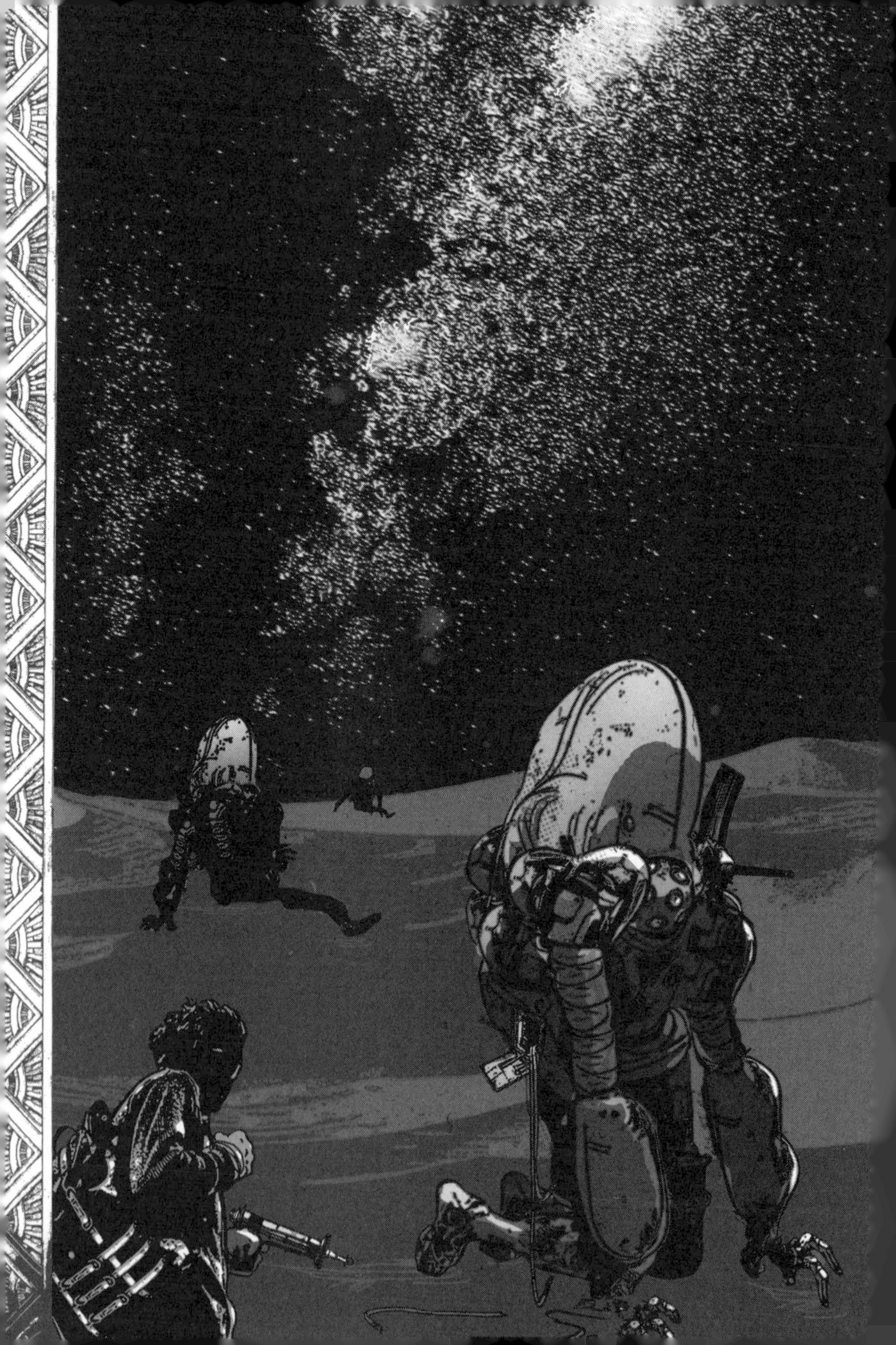

//SLEEPINGGIANTS//

Kerion could tell from the lack of weathering that the mammoth chassis of the heavy shells had not been long in the wasteland. They were of a design he did not recognize but based on a design principle he knew very well.

When Barry climbed the first one and looked inside the pilot's pod what he found was a desiccated corpse that looked like it had been there a very long time. That didn't make sense though, because the uniform was new looking but the corpse looked like it had been there for years. There were signs that the shells had been in combat relatively recently too. But it wasn't until the third giant and the third strangely diminished corpse that Kerion noticed the holes in the filter valves. Kerion found a medrob still sealed in its sterilbag clutched in the yellowed hands of one of the pilots. He took the thing, which looked like a white, rolled up pill bug the size of a veggie burger, and put it in his pack.

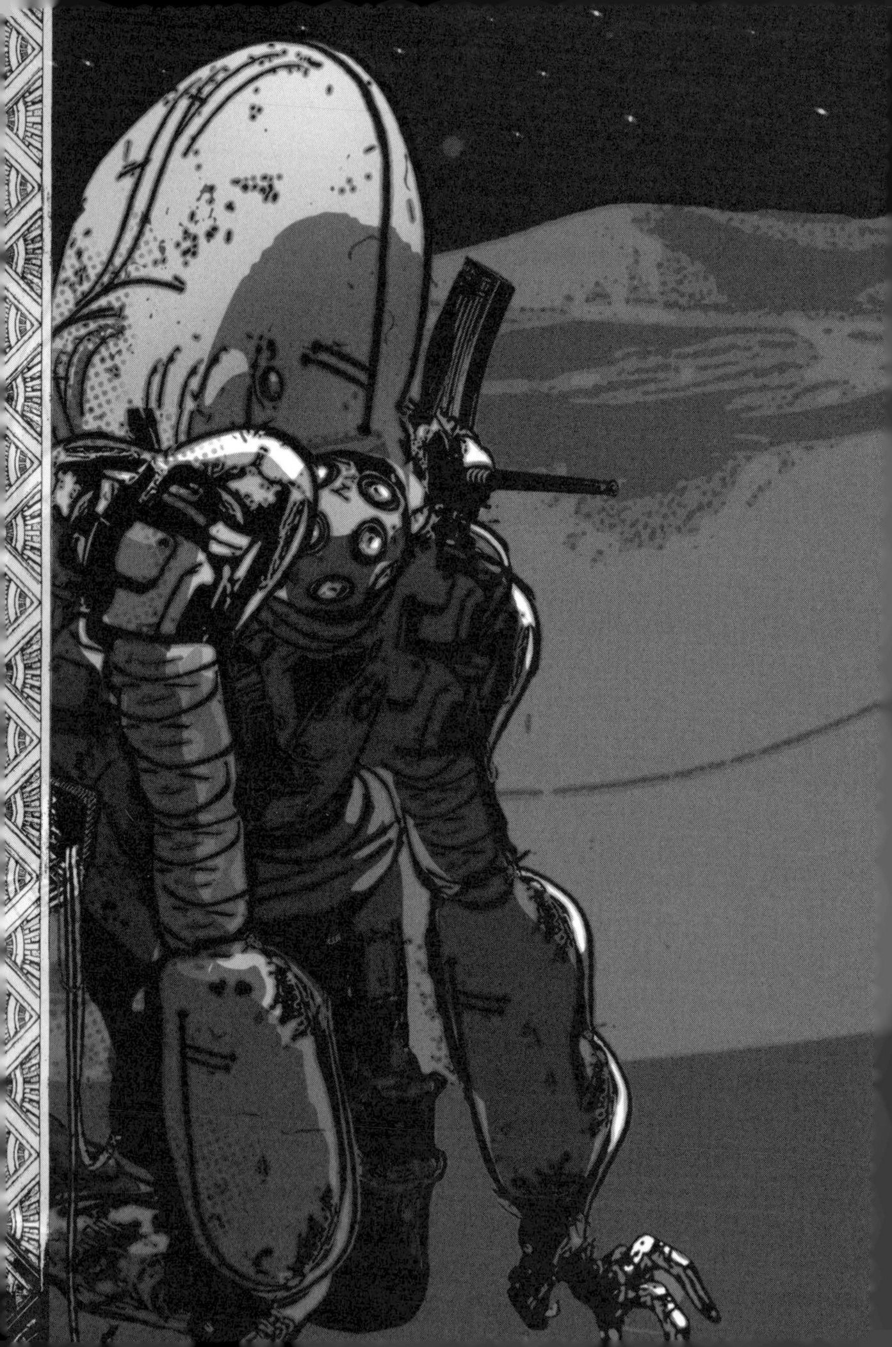

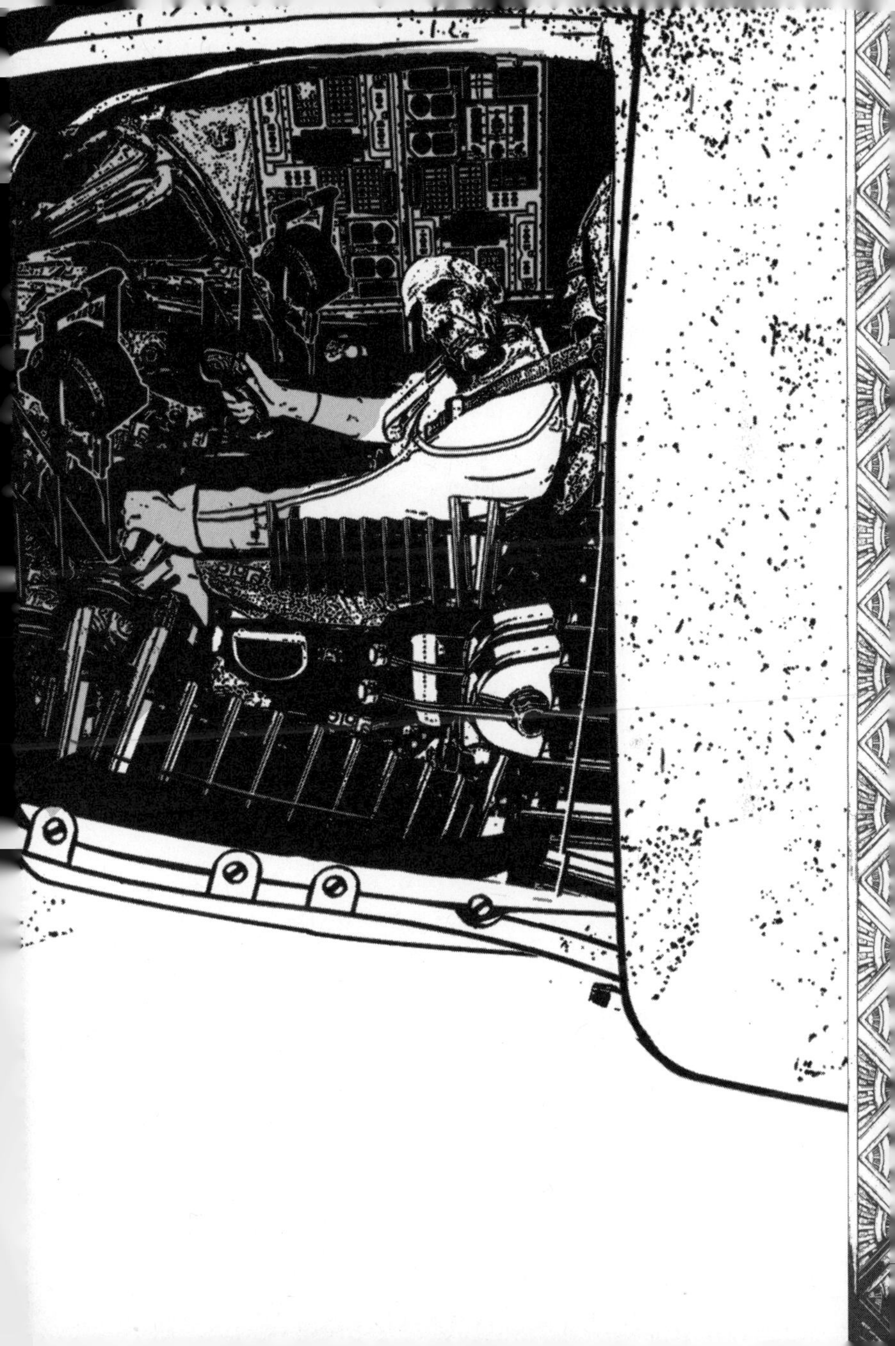

"I don't quite understand but something killed the pilots in a strange way."

They moved on and at the epicenter of the giants found a little diner automat.

"This is what they stopped for I think."

"Like that watering hole we passed with the birds."

"Yeah"

The automat looked clear, in good repair, with neon lights and music that drifted toward them. In the doorway a withered corpse in a new-looking uniform was being bumped rhythmically by the automatic door.

"Oh excuse me," the door said each time.

Barry didn't seem interested in the automat; he was looking at the giants.

"Do you think they still work?"

"Oh excuse me, Oh excuse me, Oh excuse me."

That's when they heard the scream.

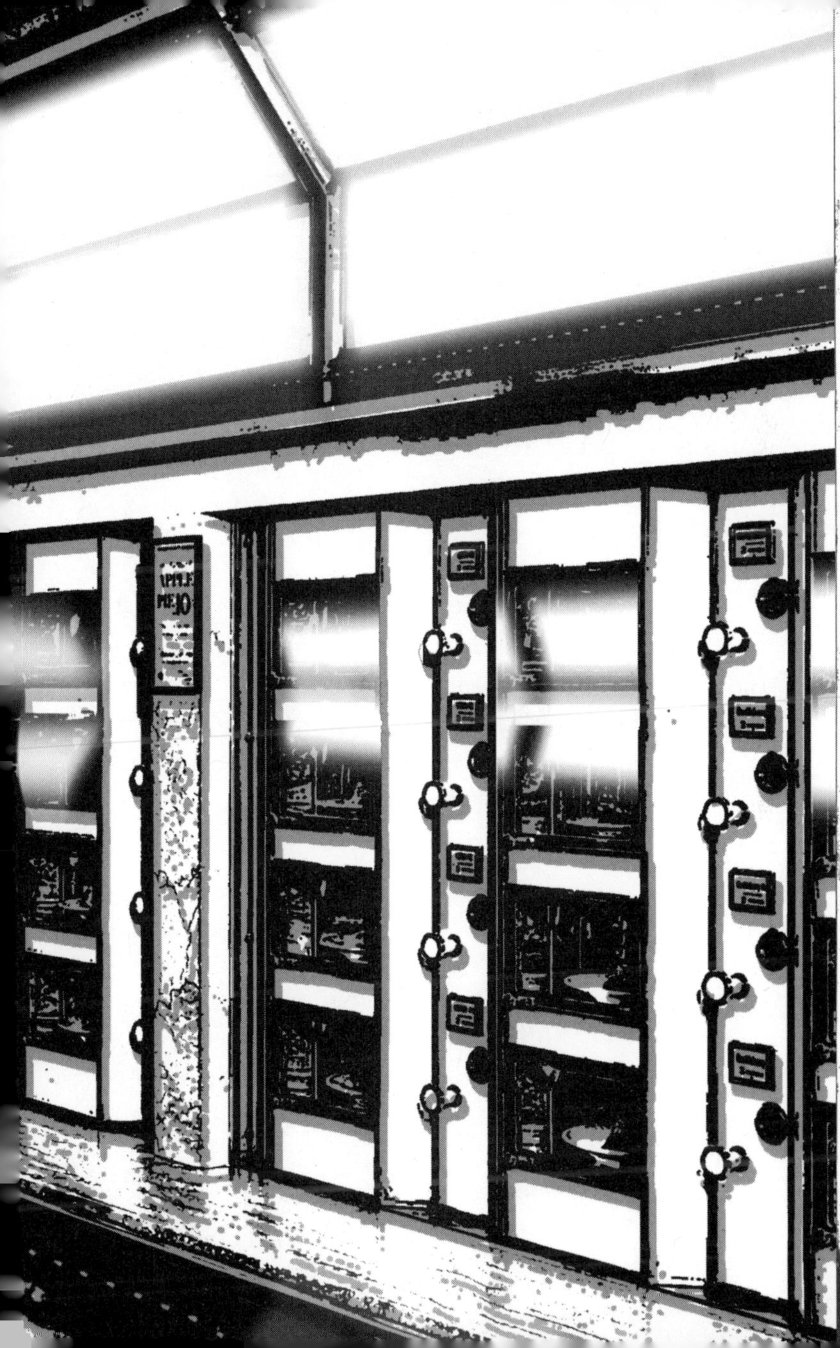
APPLE
PIE 10

//UNFOLDED//

It was a person.

A person in terrible pain.

Not far away amid the giants they could make out what must be a pilot, lying on the ground at the feet of the squat heavy shell. The pilot screamed again, writhing in agony. The pilot reached toward them, then waved them off angrily.

"Wait," Kerion said as Barry was about to run toward him.

"Dad?"

"Look. Look there."

The autovolt was perfectly still because that's how they always were if they weren't moving. A person, even one trying to be still is never completely still; the autovolts become inanimate objects. It was standing amid the wreckage, tucked in but upright amid the coils of spilled machine innards. They saw it move just its hand suddenly. The pilot screamed again.

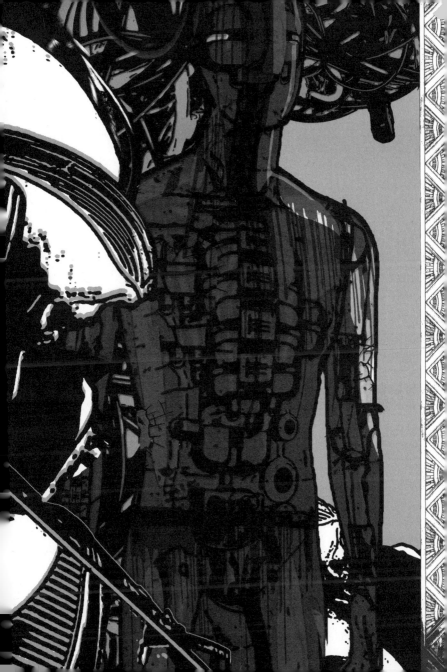

"It's hurting him."

"I know."

"We have to help."

"I know."

"Dad. It's just one. Come on."

"Barry, I think—"

Barry was already moving; he had the bow unfolded and had set an arrow.

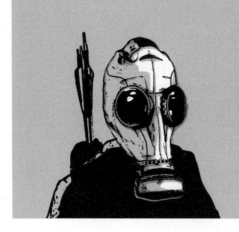

//SLIPPERY//

"I ask respectfully that you give me the box," the autovolt said.

It stood amid the guts of the fallen shell. The giant had been partially and forcefully disassembled, creating a hollow. In that space was the autovolt. Coolant pattered on its smooth surface, a drop at a time, from somewhere over its head.

"YA nikogda ne sdelayu etogo Lozhnyy chelovek" the pilot said. *I'll never do it, false man.*

The autovolt pulled on a thin copper wire that was hooked carefully through the muscle of the man's leg like a cruel fishhook.

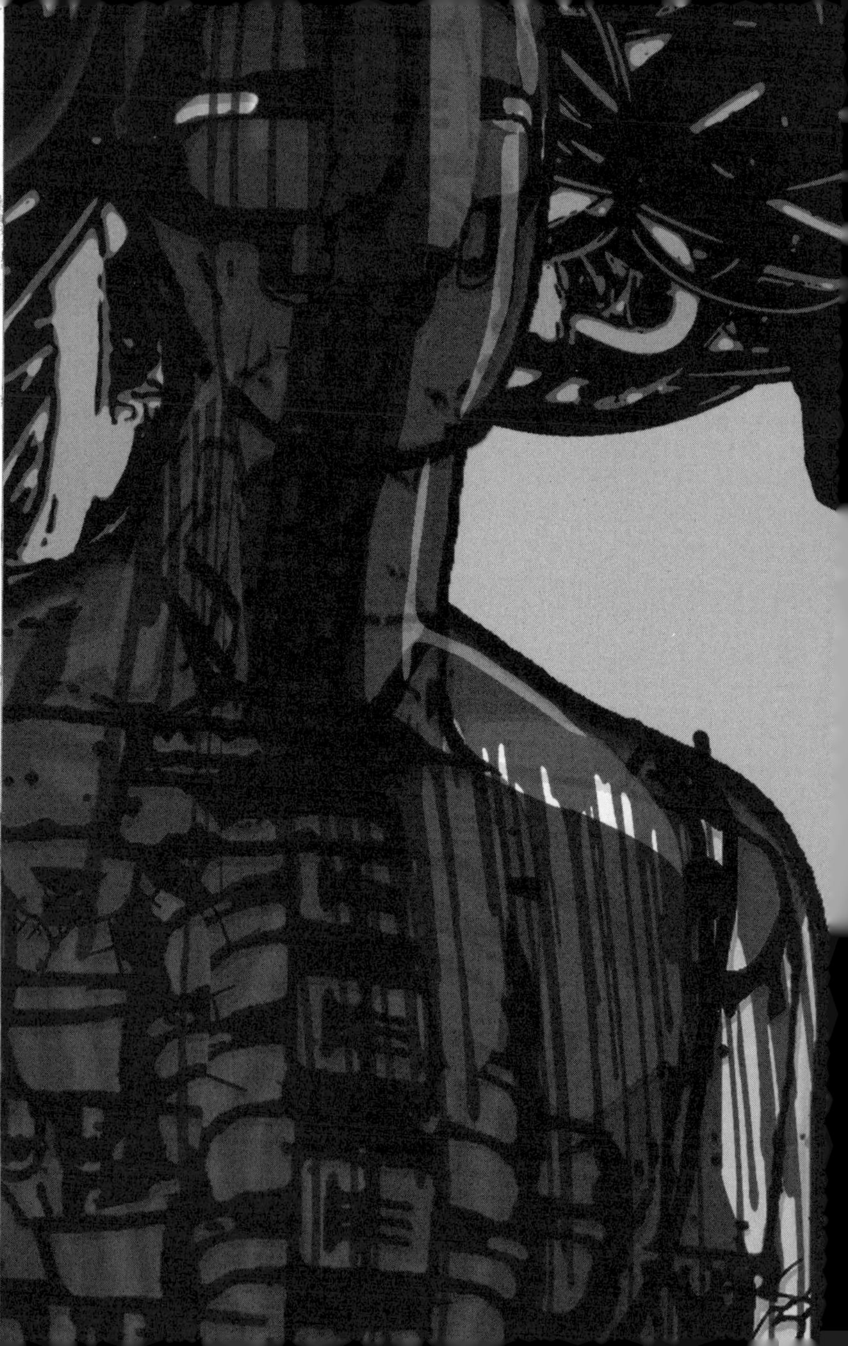

"Eventually one of the others will come to help you and I will ask them in your place."

"Oni vse mertvy, lzhivyy chelovek" the pilot said and laughed. *They are all dead false man.*

Kerion walked up slowly and deliberately.

The autovolt politely declared, "I am Unit 11389865-43. Identify yourself."

"I am unit 8347-34."

"Incorrect, you are a human occupant."

"Exchange to verify," Kerion said.

"Exchange to verify," Unit 11389865-43 said.

Kerion lifted his jacket and shirt, took the retracted power cable by its grip, and passed it to the autovolt. The autovolt's hands, slippery from the coolant, closed. The cable popped free.

"Exchange to verify," Slippery said.

Kerion took the cable again evenly and passed it to Slippery. It tried to grasp it in the rubberized pads of its fingertips, but again the slick cable popped free.

"Exchange to verify."

Kerion took the cable again evenly and passed it to Slippery. It tried to grasp it in its hand but again the slick fingers popped the cable out.

"Exchange to verify," Slippery said. Kerion took the cable again, passed it to the autovolt and the forced drama continued when the cable popped free of the automatic fingers.

//KARTA//

Barry watched as his father tried very hard to remain calm and carefully repeat each action. He passed the cable to Slippery, who dropped it. He passed the cable to Slippery, who dropped it. If he sighed, if he acted annoyed, if he swore in frustration, the autovolt would be free of its Ident Protocol and would attack. It would kill his father with bare hands.

The pilot began to laugh. It was painful for him—Barry could tell from the flinching after each guffaw—but the laughter built with each repeated action of Slippery and Kerion's absurd loop.

The pilot held the cartridge aloft toward Kerion.

"Karta," he said. *Map*.

//SANDWICHSANDWICH SOUPDESSERT//

Barry raced toward the automat away from his father, the pilot and Slippery. He bounded over the corpse that had fallen in the door then looked about.

"Oh excuse me, Oh excuse me, Oh excuse me," the door continued.

There was another corpse on a chair and another on the floor. The perfect wall of selectable food items glittered here though. All of them were freshly replaced today. Barry dug into his pockets to produce a handful of tokens. He moved across the menu surface depositing coins. Sandwich, Sandwich, Soup, Dessert Cake, Dessert Pie, Ice cream. Plunk, plunk, plunk went the coins from his shaking fingers. Then he ran to the jukebox and selected a dozen songs by running his hands down both rows of indicators. Then Barry spun toward the window booth, reached past the corpse of a pilot, and pushed the button for a coffee refill.

Barry slipped as he pivoted on the polished checker-board floor to run for the door. He crashed to his knees but scrambled forward. The pilot's body was there, a strange thin grinning thing in loose haptic coveralls. Barry made it back to his feet grabbing at the door jamb. He didn't stop to look toward his father and Slippery. He ran, fast and straight as he could behind the sightline of the mechanical giants.

//WITHER//

"Possible human occupant detected. Discontinue protocol," Slippery said.

The autovolt released the copper wire, stepped forward at once and Kerion stepped backward out of its way, resisting the urge to grab it, to attack. Slippery had an odd attachment to its chassis that Kerion had never seen before. A canister and grip nozzle that seemed to have been built as a specialized attachment for its arm. Slippery turned toward where Barry was hiding and began to walk.

As Slippery passed the pilot, who was still extending the cartridge in Kerion's direction, the autovolt raised the strange attachment and it sputtered. Only a few drops came free, but they hit the pilot. He was silent at once and began to wither.

//BOX//

As Slippery trotted off toward the automat diner, Kerion took a long deep breath. He was trying so hard to trust Barry's back-up plan. Facing the danger was always easier than waiting while his son did. Then Barry was there, breathing hard from the run.

"Okay, let's get him out of here… oh no."

"He's gone. We've got to move though, Slippery will be back."

"What's *he* holding up?"

"It's a voice box, I think," said Kerion.

"Can I take it?" Barry said.

It was clutched in the clawed yellowed flesh of the pilot's hand, the white plastic cartridge casing spotted with that same spilled coolant.

"If he'll let you."

They had other rules too. They never broke the fingers. If the dead held fast, they left it, whatever it was.

The cartridge came free easily.

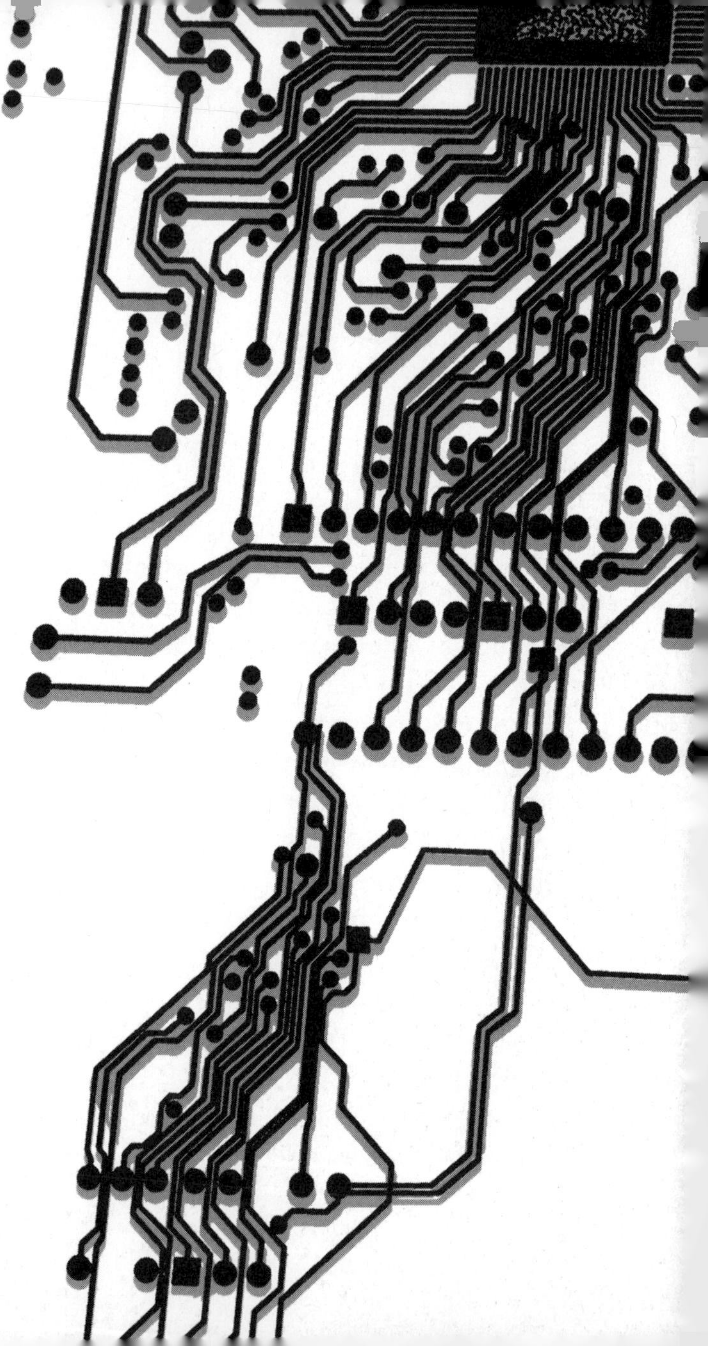

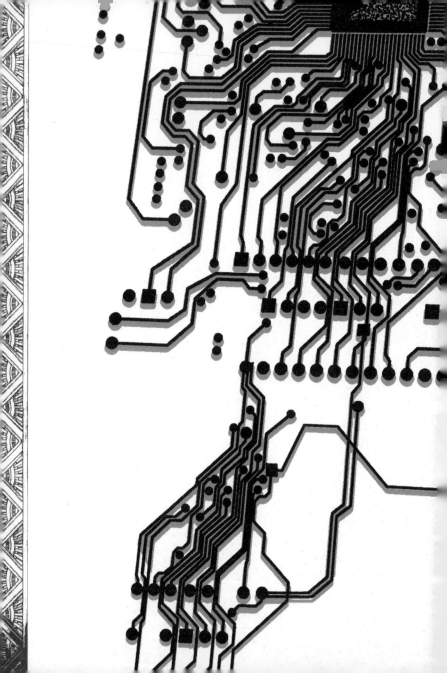

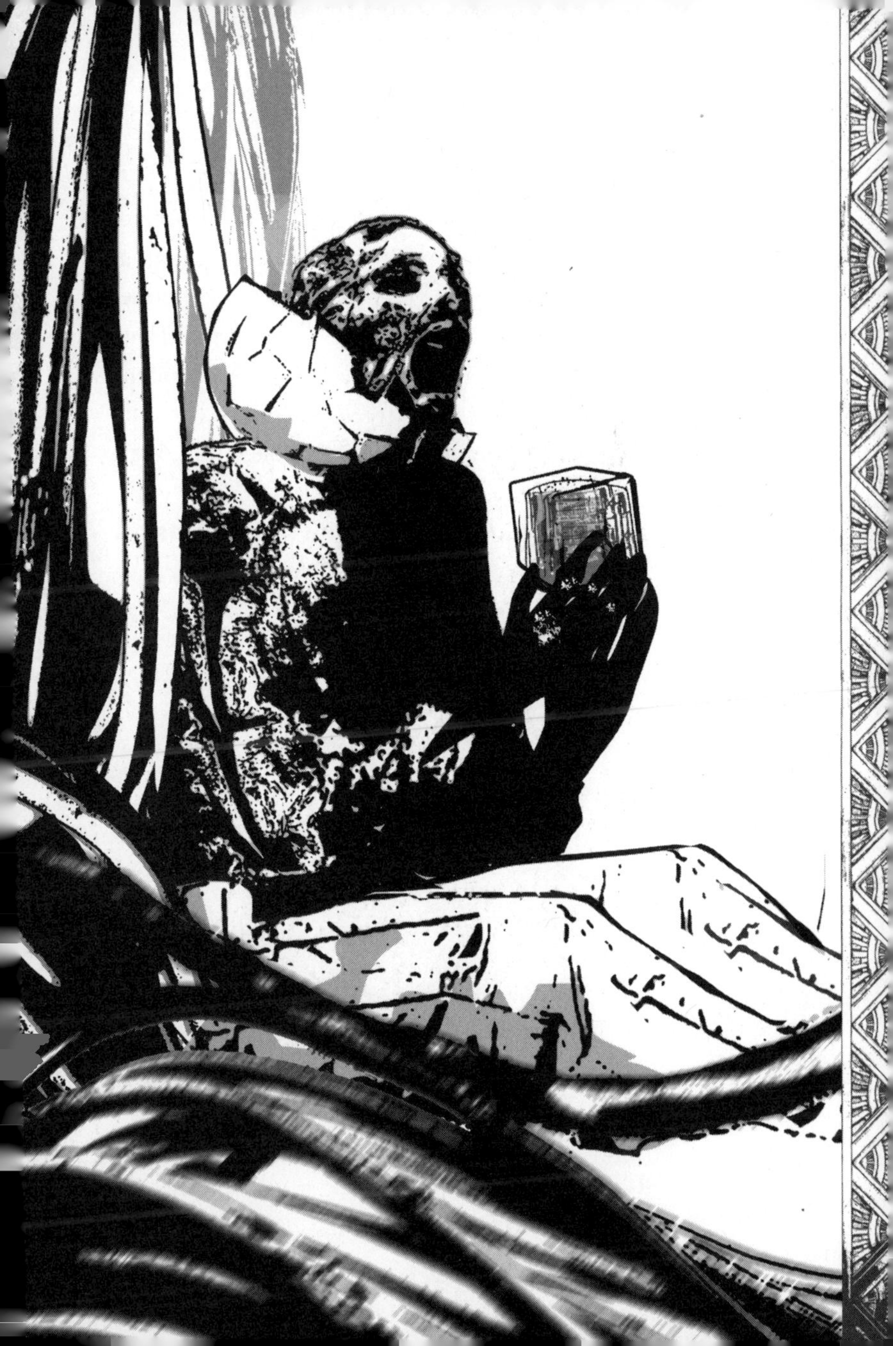

There in the pilot's hands under the box was a folded photo, with magnetic edge clips. It was a photo of a young man. The sort of thing you keep to remember someone, even though they are all grown up now. A little sliver of the past pressed to the photo paper, soiled by spilled coolant. Under that was a small paper envelope. Barry left the photo and letter there, curling the fingers back to hold it.

"We've got to go fast now, are you ready?"

Barry nodded his head, tightening his backpack straps.

//THESLIP//

They ran as fast as they could towards the elevator and the community at its base. It was a green paradise ahead or the wastes behind. Kerion needed volts and they both needed food and water.

There was a low wall which had been breached by a quadrupedal transport vehicle. The four-legged truck was half in and half out of the broken barricade. They crawled under its axle and into the community.

There was a line of causeways and they picked the one with the most trees and public art for cover. There was a line of statues more than a kilometre long, bronze figures of inventors and innovators. All of them marching in the direction of the space elevator in a silent, frozen procession of progress.

Knowing that running alone was not going to help them if Slippery was still following them, Kerion and Barry took shelter under the shadow of a statue of Loni Motts, creator of the first automatic heart. Kerion checked his weapon. The ray pistol had three discharges left of five original cells. It had been full when the woman on the Last Train had used it on Kerion. The weapon had not been made to be used this way. It was effective against people but it needed a sustained beam to cut down an autovolt. Two to four charges usually, depending on the range.

Once an autovolt was hit by something, they changed directions rapidly, so it was hard to keep the beam on one from far off. Kerion had witnessed the effect of the autovolt's canister weapon on the pilot. He didn't dare get close again.

They knew that the thoroughness of the autovolt meant that if it hadn't seen them leave, it would begin a systematic search from the automat. Slippery would keep looking, following protocols efficiently. Once it set a perimeter, it would expand it until it found a sign of them. Their footprints would be easy to follow, but maybe the blowing dust out there would hide them. Because of the way it had disengaged from him, Kerion believed he might still use the autovolt Ident Protocol against it.

"Take this," he said to Barry, handing him the raygun. He carefully extended his abdominal cable. He wiped the cable clean with his shirt, then allowed it to retract, then repeated the action.

They waited awhile under the growing heat of the high sun, sipping warm juice from scavenged bottles.

Slippery never arrived.

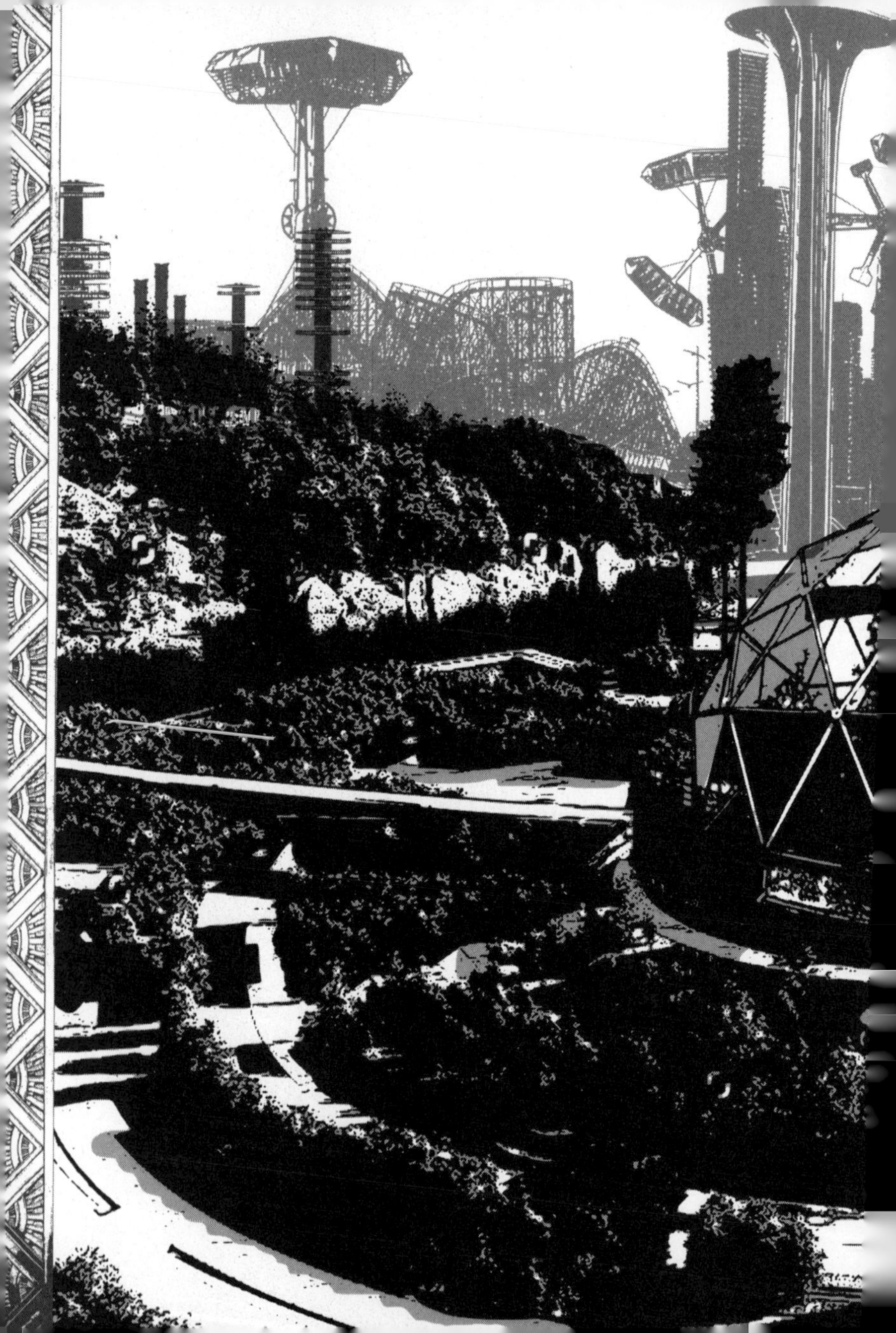

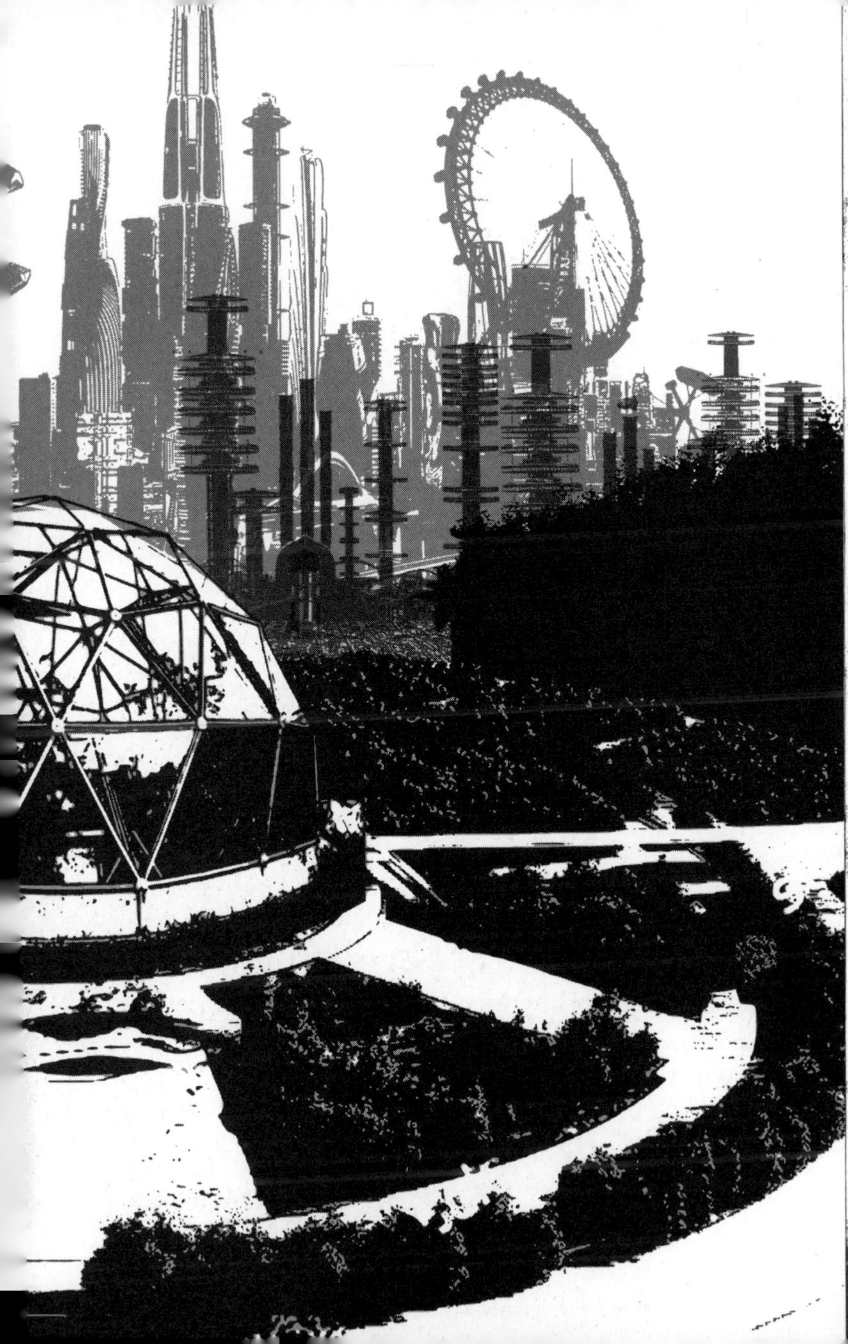

//VOICE?//

"There's a voice in here?" Barry asked, hefting the white box the pilot had 'given them'.

"Yes."

"How does it work?"

"I don't really know. I mean I know the answer is that it's an intelligent algorithm, but I honestly don't know *how* it works."

"You heard voices in the war though?"

"Yes. The Jet Jumper Shells all had voices, but they were very…"

"Very what?"

"Very specialized. A bit narrow minded. Development tried to give them interests later, something to talk about besides work."

"What did yours talk about?"

Kerion paused, then smiled.

"She liked old movies."

"Billy Theodore had one in a stuffed Funny Bunny.

It taught spelling and history and always wanted to dig around for bugs and chase butterflies."

"Hmmm."

"Are you listening?"

"Yeah, sure."

"What is it?"

"I looked like, well, it looked like Slippery was talking to that person."

"What were they saying?"

"I have no idea. I couldn't really hear it. But I'm sure they were saying something."

"What do you think *this* one talks about?"

"Well, it was important for that pilot to hold it in the end, but we aren't likely to find out."

"Why not?" He looked at the edges, smooth except for the recessed socket port.

"Doesn't have a body. No mouth, no voice."

"Oh." Then, "What sort of body does it need?"

"Well, let's look. See there, that's the port connection. Any automatic with a connection port to match—that's a D9 I think, so military or security, though a few civilian models might have it."

"*Then* it would talk?"

"Then whatever you plugged it into would become its body."

"Do you think maybe it was just…"

"Just?"

"Just his friend. Maybe it came from his shell, maybe he just didn't want it to be alone."

Kerion lifted the cube from the boy's hands. Looked at it very carefully.

"Our voices, when we had them, moved from shell to shell with us, so that's possible. Some of the crews got really attached to theirs. But this looks so new. Yeah, look here, the port seal is still on."

There was a little tab of clear resin over the connection port that Barry hadn't noticed; it kept dust and grit out of the connection. At school long ago, Kit, a kid a year ahead of him, had had a habit of sticking fresh port connectors under his chair. Somehow, he'd figured out the blind spot of the cleaning units and kept putting his chair there at the end of day. After a term of lesson units, he'd created a little pattern of the resin dots. Then one day someone must have moved the chair, just a bit out of the blind spot, and it was cleaned of all that careful work. Kit had never tried again.

Barry pressed his thumb into the resin.

"Can I keep it?"

"Will you carry it?"

"Yeah."

"*Keep what you can carry.*" They both said in unison and then laughed.

//MANYHANDS//

The community and structures around the base of the Backbone of Night were ringed by an immense green space. Kerion and Barry approached the high wall, it was maybe five hundred meters tall. They could see places where rail lines and freeways intersected. What caught their attention was a section of the wall that had fallen down.

Kerion had grabbed Barry and pulled him down flat.

There was a collapsed section with a parkland on the far side, and the largest number of autovolts they had ever seen in one place.

Autovolts were pulling up slabs of ferrocrete and passing down a line a thousand robots long. One hand to the other, a conveyor belt of hands. With its hands free, the Front Worker began to claw at the ground, then the line of autovolts shuffled again and something was being passed hand to hand and into the hole. Small stones filled the bottom, then a hundred handfuls of black earth passed a palmful at a time filled the hole with perfect efficiency.

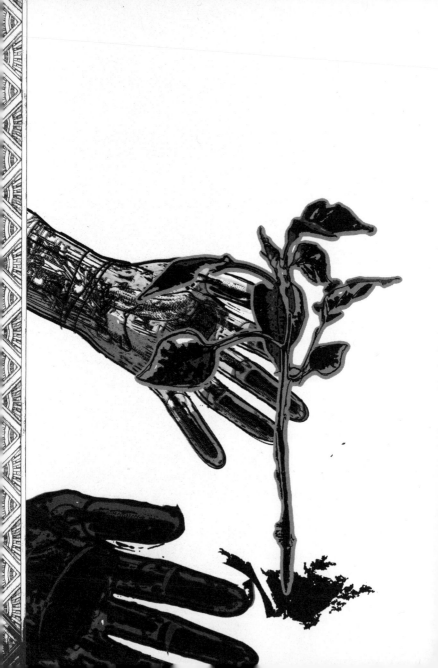

Then at last a single object, which the autovolts took great care to pass between them like a child passed down a line of one thousand cautious parents. The Front Worker placed a young and green sapling into its planting bed. The Line shifted and a dozen pails of water made their way to the tree down the autovolt system.

"Many hands make light work," Kerion said.

"They're planting trees!"

"It's weird to see them working."

"Maybe, maybe things are changing?"

"Maybe."

"But you doubt it."

"I doubt it."

//ONCEHELD//

They had found a sort of entry port. A place with a thousand podcars stacked up like pearls against the wall. There were shops and a multi-level mall, promenade, and viewing stations. The power was on, and a song was playing. *Funny Funny Funny fun fun funny hop along hop along goes the funny bunny—*

"Can we stop here?"

"If you want, but—"

"I have an idea."

The Funny Landing Cartoons kiosk had been stocked with perpetual toys, little robotic wonders that danced or sang or helped you clean your room. Barry took out the cube and checked the port, then moved amid the toys, picking a few up and examining their connections. A Danger Duck waddled up to him and said, "We've got to help Mega Mouse—" But Barry knocked it away discouraged.

Kerion knew the cube wasn't a toy and that the connection wouldn't fit. He admired the idea and the attempt so waited patiently, keeping a lookout.

Kerion scanned the perfection and glittering chrome of the promenade, its signs and symbols. There had been fighting here, awful fighting.

Every perfect boulevard and shop and cafe on the promenade that seemed unaffected by the horrors of not so long ago told a story if you knew what to look for. Newly built things everywhere. Perfect and polished and without wear. But not everything was new. A slight loss of luster on the candy-coated surfaces, still nice but not new. Everything new meant it had been replaced before it was maintained. Everything that had been replaced had been damaged. The perfection was a sign of calamity.

There were also a few blind spots the repairs had missed. Little places just out of reach of the web of protocols that overlay the automatic world. Just there between a corner of the counter and the edge of the door was a bit of detritus that told a specific type of tale. Kerion bent and picked it up, a plastic casing that had once held a bullet.

//CRAVEPILLS//

They didn't call it the 7th then. Wars don't have a name at the start. When you are in them at the beginning you don't even know it is a war, it's just what's happening, and you react to it. It's just cause and effect clicking together like tipped-over dominos on their way down the line. Something is there that shouldn't be, and so you are sent. Then you achieve the stated goal, or you don't, and the next day there is another thing to do. Even the term day becomes relative because, slick on stimulants, you slide from day to day without rest.

The shell becomes your skin, and you are just a soft part of a hard machine. You begin to forget what touching your own skin feels like, then one day while the shell is in the bay and you are in your rack, your own feet slide against each other and you wake believing you are not alone. Then you begin to resent rest and time without your shell and crave the pills and crave the security of the machine. You forget that it isn't secure at all because you

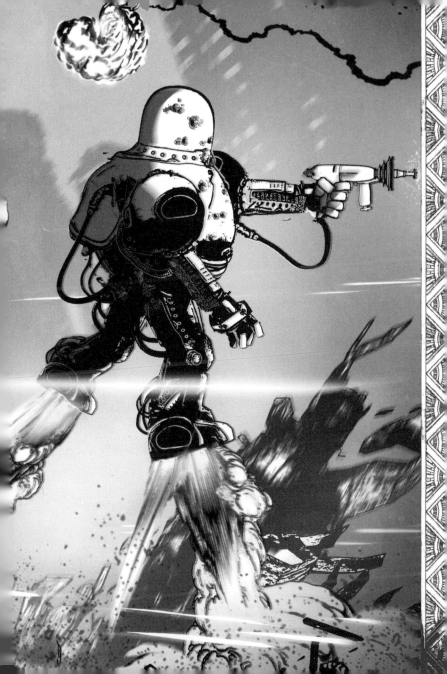

are being deployed into an arena of death machines all designed, just as yours is, to allow the pilots a chance to crack that shell and get at the soft meat inside.

The Jet Jumpers weren't heavily armored compared to the rest of The Line. They were fast though, dropping in and leaping out. In dreams when you fall a great distance, you often wake before you land. But Kerion had memories, not dreams, of long falls into fire and shrapnel where he landed and contributed to the shrapnel and fire before leaping away. He'd had the experience of landing from a fall of such a great height so many times that he dreamed of falling and hitting the ground all the time, without waking up.

//CHRISTMASTREE//

There were a lot of odd things hanging from the trees. A bicycle, a radio, an open cooler hanging by its handle, a dozen or so individual balloons, a belt, a pair of spectacles, a raven's wing, a shoe, a child's toy train, an umbrella, a watch. In the higher branches, Barry saw a little bot, no bigger than an infant, rounded and chromed with long arms and prehensile hands and feet. It was dragging an office chair into the higher branches, but it was ungainly, catching on the branches and causing the top of the tree to sway.

"It looks like it was activated for the holiday, but no one had put out the decorations."

"So, it just found things to hang up? I didn't think a simple bot like that could intuit a response.'

"Oh no, I doubt that it did, I think that it misinterpreted its regular programming and took what was nearest to the regular decoration box, and when no one told it not to, it simply kept at it. It just keeps taking the nearest object up in the tree to decorate it."

"They just have to do what they were built to do."

"Yeah, we've talked about that a lot."

"Us too, I guess."

"How do you mean?"

"Just, well, we're afraid to die, so we keep running from it, and I guess that's what we're made to do."

Kerion stopped and dropped his pack. "Is that what you think we're doing? Running from death?"

"Aren't we?"

"Oh son, no. We're living. We're running toward a life. Out there, out there is a place where you will find happiness and rest and love and family. I believe that with all my heart."

"You said praying is a silly superstition."

"It is."

"Then what is the difference? What you hope will happen isn't real or likely or even possible. It's a myth."

"No son," Kerion said, picking up his pack. "It's a plan."

//FALLBACK//

"What are all of these?"

"Automatics, I guess. Don't touch them. They've all been in fights. Lots of fights."

"But with who?"

"Someone overrode their primary protocols with a protective one, I guess. We've never seen this before. Plenty of corrupted automatics become dangerous. Locks that don't open, cars that won't stop, but nothing that could make you an army."

"I think there was a last stand here. That this was a fall-back point," Barry said.

"Fall back to where? Oh!" Kerion said, spinning round to look at the Backbone, then he followed it up with his eyes until it disappeared into the blue of the sky.

"Strategic withdrawal." Kerion looked to the tower as well, squinting more as his gaze rose. "I mean it makes sense. Nothing we've seen or experienced suggests that the autovolts destroy infrastructure to achieve their objective. In a conventional war, that giant string would be an easy target. But the autovolts don't have heavy weapons, just numbers and a simple goal. I think, maybe whatever did all this"—Kerion pointed to the glittering new causeway and shops—"was a last stand while the rest went up the elevator."

"So…"

"So I guess that's what we'll try to do too."

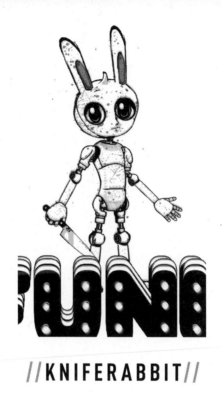

//KNIFERABBIT//

"What is it?"

"It's Hop Happy the Funny Bunny, but not the one I know from the show. Something took off its fuzzy parts."

"It's looking around, just like—oh, here it comes."

"Oh, hello there I'm—"

The cartoon rabbit came toward them with a knife and Kerion didn't hesitate. He burned the thing's head hollow with two charges from the raygun.

//MUSEUM//

"What is supposed to be here?"

"Lots of cultural artifacts from different eras."

"The displays are mostly empty."

"I guess someone took everything. Historians are like that I've been told."

//PNEUMAIL//

The Pneumatic Mail center reminded Barry of the Zieth Concert Hall he had gone to with his mother. It was a beautiful edifice of sweeping arches and polished brass. The building itself also had parts that looked like the automatic pipe organ pizza parlor he used to have birthdays at. Incoming lines from the Funny Land community were easy to see sweeping together in a rather ostentatious fan of glittering brass and clear tubes. It was the outgoing lines that caught Barry and Kerion's attention.

The pneumatic tubes had all been shattered or leveraged out of alignment until their seals cracked. Hundreds of broken arteries that led out toward the horizon.

"What do you think happened here?"

Amid the debris of the tubes were shovels, axes, prybars all strewn about.

"Not sure. It's a bit strange. Look, the tools were just cast aside after this, that's not really like an autovolt. Plus they don't tend to smash apart anything that doesn't have a person inside."

They found evidence of defecation and some food waste.

"People did this."

"Look here, someone put all the message tubes in here and burned them." Inside a wheelbarrow that had served as an improvised firepit was a mass of melted plastics and charred bits of paper. There was a pile of repair pod robots, all of them looking like they had been smashed apart by those same axes and shovels.

Curiosity brought them round to the entrance of The Pneumatic Mail Center.

"What's inside?"

"It's the pneumailroom. Sorting automatics and likely a few sending hatches."

Someone had written, BAD THOUGHTS BRING BAD THINGS in very neat and very careful red stencil adhesive. All around the front door were smashed cleaning robots that had come to remove the vandalism.

"Whoever did that was afraid to go in."

"Can we go in?"

"We shouldn't."

"But you want to."

"I want to, yeah."

At full speed a pneumail room was a thing to behold. Kerion had seen them many times. His father had liked to bring him and they would just watch the lightning speed and precision of the automatic world coming into its infancy.

Everything was quiet here though, and Kerion realized that he had no memory of this sort of machine like this, still and waiting.

The sorting robot had performed a Sisyphean task of keeping what appeared to be a slow but steady stream of pneumail from getting disorganized after the outgoing tubes became inoperable. Once it had run out of station slots, it had simply begun lining them up on the floor to the limit of its reach. There were thousands of them. Just then, the tube *fwoomped* and another arrived. The pneumail robot whirled into action. Precise manipulators shot along ceiling tracks and collected the tube, scanned the barcode and then sped it to its place amid the rows on the floor.

"Where did that come from?"

"I think we know."

"The tower. Let's open it."

"If we try to tamper with this system, it will defend itself."

"That's why whoever ruined it didn't come in. But why break it at all? Maybe they were protecting people from whatever those messages are?"

"Maybe."

Kerion's abdomen chimed.

"I'm low," he said.

They moved on.

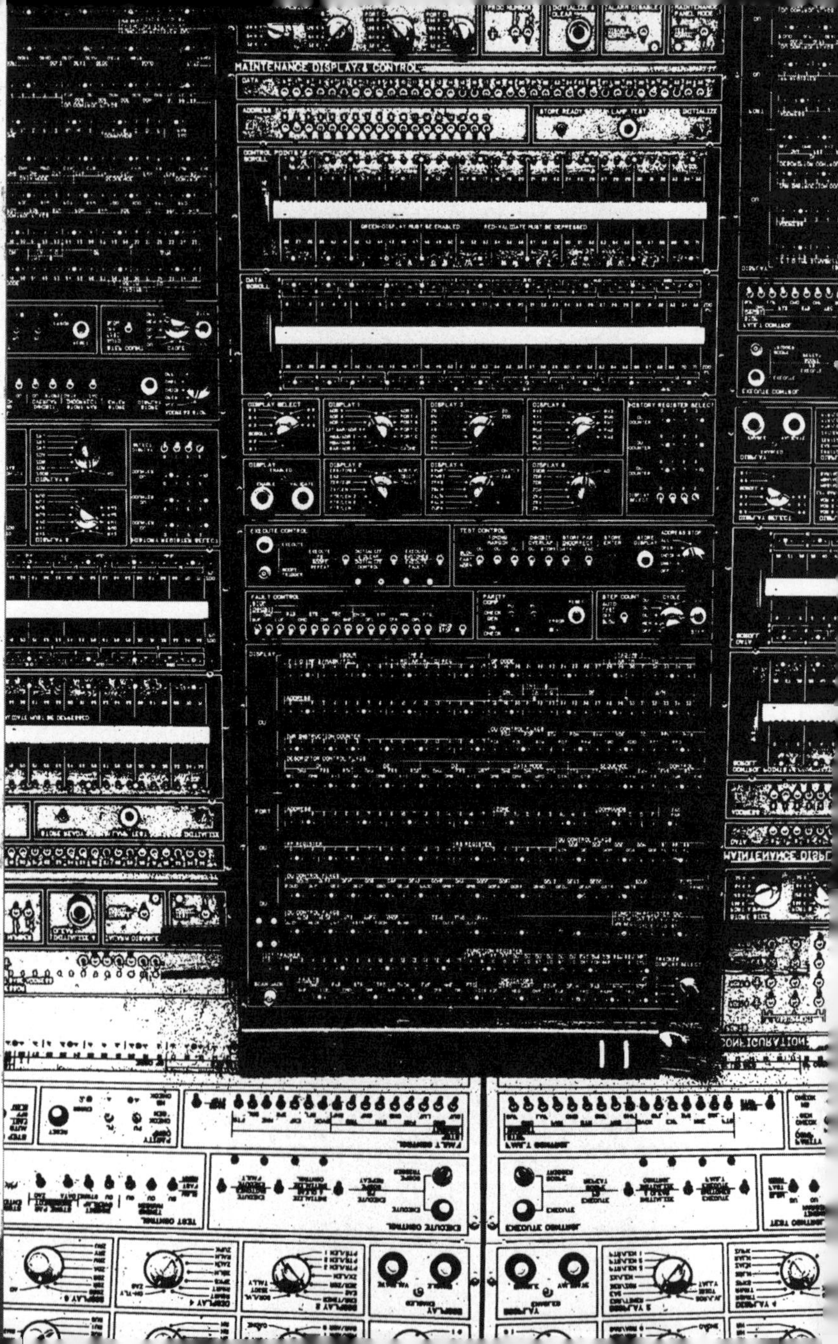
MAINTENANCE DISPLAY & CONTROL
DATA
ADDRESS
STORE READY
LAMP TEST
INITIALIZE
CONTROL POINTS SCROLL
DATA SCROLL
DISPLAY SELECT
DISPLAY 1
DISPLAY 2
DISPLAY 3
DISPLAY 4
DISPLAY 5
DISPLAY 6
HISTORY REGISTER SELECT
DISPLAY ENABLED
ENABLE
VALIDATE
EXECUTE CONTROL
TEST CONTROL
FAULT CONTROL
PARITY
STEP COUNT
CYCLE
DISPLAY
CONFIGURATION

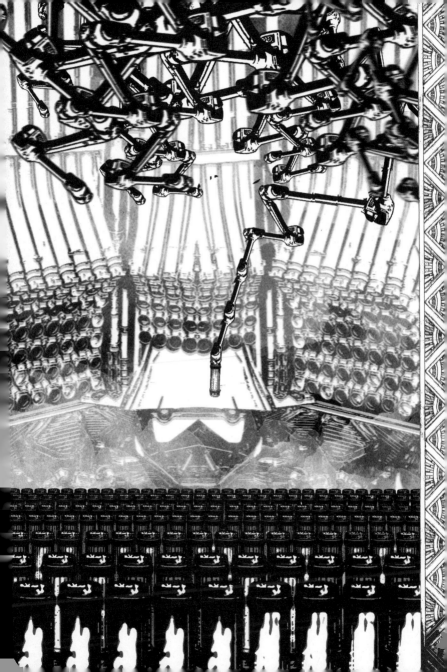

//VOICEBOX//

It was the whirring of functioning cleaning robots that attracted their attention. A dozen little round floor polishers were bumping into each other and into a damaged power armor that protruded from the floor like a bug half caught in amber.

The chassis had been re-concreted into the floor, it almost looked like a statue. Some past explosion had carved out a huge portion of the street and the repair robot had filled it in smooth. Now an army of robots that cleaned floors were doing their very best to work around it.

"What is that!?"

"Careful."

The chassis was open, unfolded, and looked like a huge robotic man that had been turned inside out.

"If you look there, in the service panel, you see it?"

"No," Barry said.

"Okay see that blue bundle of cable?"

"Yeah."

"Follow that to the red box then look—"

"A voice box!" Barry said, taking off his pack with excitement and digging inside. "Can we switch 'em?"

"Maybe, it depends on why this suit is here. The mantle usually has a backup battery, not enough to power the suit if the main cell is flat but enough to run a voice diagnostic."

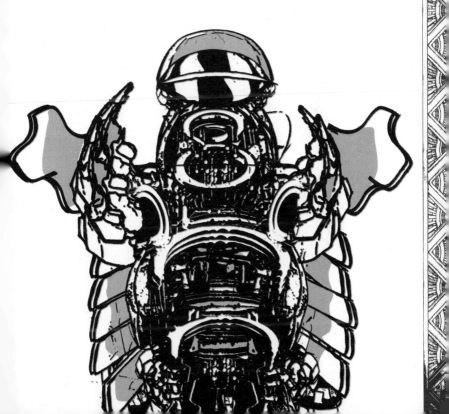

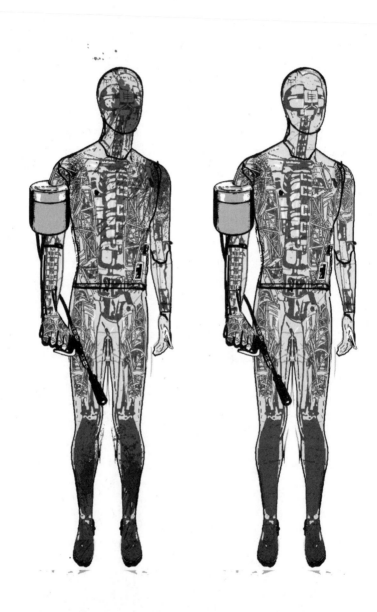

"It might have enough power to talk to us!"

"Don't get your hopes up. If this rig is here, it's likely damaged somehow that I can't see. But *maybe* us and your little pal can have a chat," Kerion said, nodding to the white cube.

//ORIGAMI//

"There you go. Just slide in."

"I don't like how it feels. You do it."

"I can't do it, not with these legs, but you can do it."

Kerion lowered Barry into the shell. He had checked its diagnostics and the machine armor was sound.

Barry noticed an autovolt at the moment his dad began to let go.

"Dad!"

Kerion spun, grabbing for the ray gun.

"Make a fist!" Kerion yelled.

Barry thumbed the control studs inside the thumbs of the huge gauntlets. Tink Tink Tink Tink. The plating began to close tight beginning at his ankles. The autovolt marched forward, then began the run, calculating the situation. Its arm came up, the bayonet in its forearm flipped out, and the autovolt dove and plunged forward. Clink, the armor snapped shut on the blade, snapping it off, the point an inch deep inside Barry's abdomen.

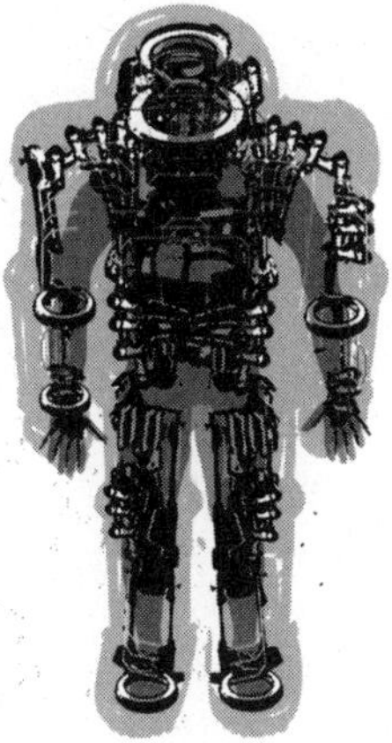

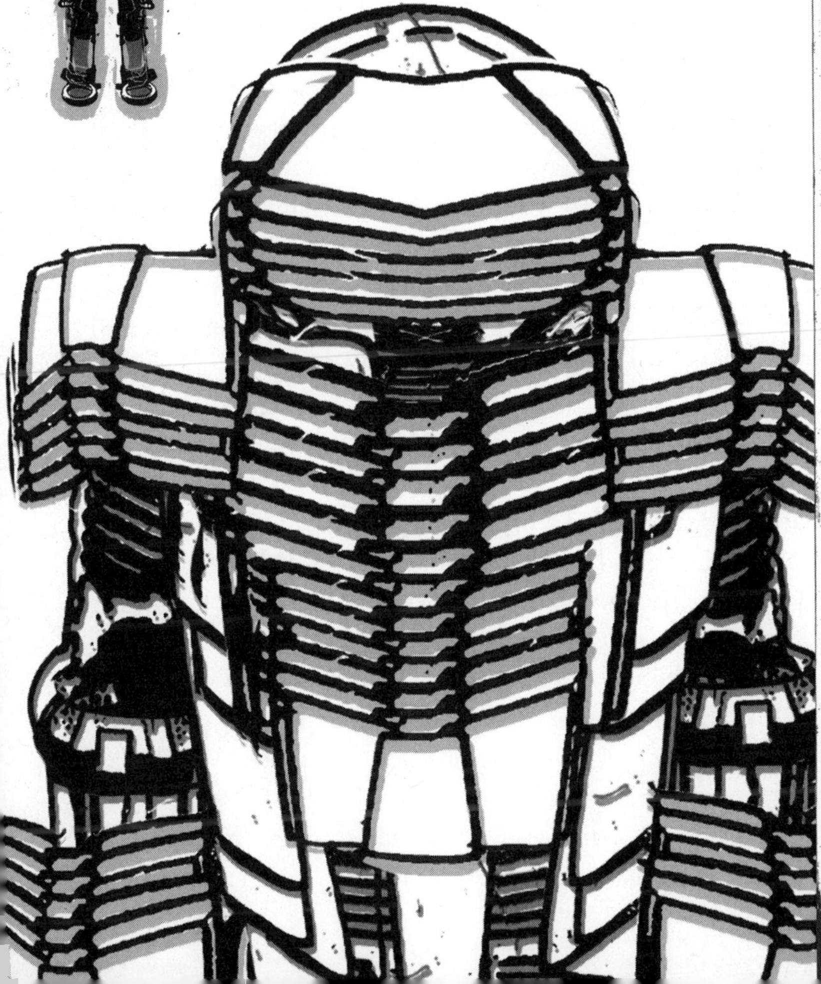

Barry screamed and flailed inside the suit, worsening the wound. He swatted at his stomach as if stung by a hornet, panicked. The pain and the enclosure and the rage and the helplessness spun him like a gyroscope. He writhed, and the haptics of the suit gripped him. The pain was wilding, and he beat the ground and at his trapped legs.

"Barry, it's Dad. Barry, can you hear me?"

Then he heard it again, then again, "Son, can you hear me? Can you open it?"

The exoskeleton unfolded like origami and Kerion slid Barry from the socket, panting and gasping.

The space they had been in was obliterated as if by a bomb, shards and fragments of the autovolt scattered amid ruined shards of concrete and tiles. The chassis Barry was wearing had obliterated the autovolt, but he hadn't even felt it.

Kerion took Barry into his arms, pulling him up across his knees, off of the floor. He pushed painfully on Barry's stomach and the boy screamed and folded.

Kerion wiped palmfuls of blood from the wound trying to see it fully. The armor had closed on the knife, catching it before it could drive deeper, but the wound was severe; as the suit had moved it had dug side to side.

"Okay, okay—" Kerion said. "Here, Here."

Then he pushed.

"Dad!" Barry cried with a shriek and a cracked voice.

"I'm here, okay, hold on."

//SMALLSPACE//

Kerion turned the burner up and put a lid on the pot to boil water.

The small space was lit by a chemical strip of phosphorescence. It was from the kit. It emitted no visible light, but with the special flat-folding glasses from the medrob kit, it lit the small chamber. The medrob was for field use, made so you could tend yourself in the dark. Barry moaned and tried to roll over, but Kerion put his hand on the boy's shoulder. The medrob was clutched to the boy's abdomen, doing its work, and while it had a firm grip, rolling over on it might dislodge it. Kerion had seen that happen before, during the 7th, but those wounds were much worse.

Except they weren't. None of them had been his son.

Kerion thumbed the info strip on the medrob and checked the battery. Full. He disconnected the charging line from his own abdominal port, then checked the power levels on his own chassis. He estimated, then stood. He took out his raygun with its single charge and tucked it under the blanket with Barry. He unpacked every edible thing in all his pockets and pack and repacked them into Barry's bag. He took out the "good" folding knife and zipped it into the leg pocket of Barry's pants. He portioned out the water in their three cantinas and put one in Barry's pack and two beside his boy. Lastly, he took out the pen recorder.

"I'm going for a recharge. I love you." Then his voice broke, and he started over.

"I'm going to recharge, I shouldn't be gone long. If I am, then you'll do your best, which is already better than mine. I love you."

//SUBSETS//

Kerion looked out the scope and divided the scene before him into a mental grid. He watched carefully and counted autovolts. He didn't have enough charge to encounter one and walk on, so he had to avoid them altogether, which was now more difficult. He had a plan, though, and believed it was sound.

He made it to a FUNNY LANDING solar pillar and plugged himself in.

The autovolt came only a moment later. It had two partial arms, walked with a limp, and had a number of loose socket joints. Its one hand rattled when it moved.

"I am unit 324152436479-45."

"I am unit 8347-34."

"Incorrect. You are a human occupant."

"Exchange to verify."

"My exchange system is damaged and may be malfunctioning. Alternative confirmation available via sensorium rhythmics."

Oh shit, Kerion thought, took a breath, and said evenly, "Affirmative. My sensorium rhythmics are malfunctioning. Only conduit exchange available."

"Signaling additional unit to verify, stand by."

"Standing by," Kerion said. "Until verification I will continue to charge."

"That sounds lovely, lovely, lovely," Rattle said.

Kerion's chassis was fully charged when Rattle's new friend, Polished, came down the lane. It had a jaunty confident stride, its perfect surface gathering the morning light. It had that odd attachment on its arm with a nozzle like Slippery had used.

"I am unit Z-5623455"

That was a new designation. One Kerion had not heard of before. Or had he? Was that what Slippery had said?

"I am unit 8347-34, exchange to verify."

"Exchange to verify."

Kerion extended his cable; the autovolt took it and extended its own. It had two different dongles: one that matched his own and one that did not. He slotted the cable.

He could outrun Rattle, but Polish had that odd attachment. Undoubtedly a weapon, and Kerion was certain, new as he was, that Polish had plenty of ammunition too. On his belt Kerion had the hammer. Not enough.

"Verification complete. You are unit 8347-34, diagnostic

indicates no connection to system subsets 45 to y934, accompany me to reclamation."

Kerion disconnected. Rattle turned and limped away back to his post. Kerion had no choice but to follow Polish until he could consider another option. He had seen autovolts walking in tandem before and tried his best to get the distance right and keep pace.

They walked a kilometer or so together while Kerion tried to fathom a smooth exit. They had entered a mall, and he saw another group of two autovolts up ahead about three hundred meters. They turned and stepped onto an escalator going down. Kerion, careful not to break stride, peeked over the rail.

Slippery was standing at the bottom of the escalator.

Kerion pulled his hammer free of his belt and attacked Polish. He struck the barrel of the nozzle attachment with the hammer with his full might and felt it give a bit, which was all he could do.

He ran. Any projectile would misfire, he hoped, giving him a moment before Polish sprinted after him.

He was right that the damaged barrel disrupted the autovolts attack. But it didn't shoot bullets or flechettes. A great cloud of aerosol gas flooded out in a fan from the dented nozzle. Kerion looked over his shoulder, then he turned round the Cinema Scopes and out of view. He was fast, his legs were very fast, but the autovolt at full speed would be much faster. He pushed through the mall's revolving doors.

Kerion crossed the causeway and pushed open the door to the DailyDeli, jumped the counter and slammed against the preparation array.

"Unfortunately, there has been some mistake!" it said. "You cannot be here for health and safety reasons. Please exit this area. We make sure every meal is fresh and clean, untouched by human hands!" The deli display showed a delicious array of prepared meat substitutes, all vegetable-based protein alternatives.

Polish was at the door. It pushed it open with one hand and flooded the room with gas.

Kerion had pushed through to the package stacks in the back. He charged through the maintenance door and scattered packaging and protein tubes. There he saw the delivery cube slot and climbed over the receiving system. He pulled himself through the slot and fell headfirst to the ground by the loading carousel. He saw the heavy gas billow from the delivery port and tumble down, but he was already away.

He sprinted right, but Polish was there, just stepping into the lane. Kerion spun and went back, charging into the narrow space between the DailyDeli and the Plush Plush. He collapsed through a hedge in the shape of a swan and into the front street again. Rattle was there waiting for him.

He swung the hammer at Rattle's outstretched, damaged hand. The automatic fingers unsocketed and flopped around even as they tried to grab him. Kieron pushed the autovolt back for just an instant, then stooped and struck it with the hammer in its knee. Rattle's leg folded in and the autovolt fell.

Polish was there again. Kerion had no choices and acted too soon without a moment to think. He ducked back through the deli, back the way he had come.

The scene in the deli was very different than a moment before. Every bit of organic matter, every bit of protein derivative had gone black and began to pool as liquid.

The cleaning robs were sliding from their alcoves and the serving counter said, "I'm so sorry, valued patron but we are closed for cleaning for the next eleven minutes."

Kerion swung the door shut behind him as Polish reached for him, its arms punching through the glass to seize his pack strap. Rather than fight the pull, he pushed toward the autovolt through the glass, Polish fell backward with Kerion on top of it. Polish clapped a hand to his thigh, and if he had been human there it would have snapped his leg bone easily. Instead, Kieron's leg made a beeping sound of a pressure alarm.

Polish's other arm was caught under its own body. Kerion struck and struck with the hammer and accidently hit the canister attachment on the arm, which dented deeply but did not rupture. The nozzle end began to sputter as the pressure change forced the gas to escape.

Kerion rolled free suddenly and scrambled on all fours for a moment, then was up, then was running.

He ran round an All-igator Shoe Boutique through a merry-go-round of slowly turning Corporate Cats being chased by a Mega Mouse. Winded, Kerion put his hand up to the display window of a Velvet Fox. Then he saw that the two smaller fingers on his right hand had dissolved into a black slime that coated his forearm.

//NOTMUCH//

"I grabbed this," he said pushing a protein tube into his son's hands. "It's not much."

Kerion fashioned a set of straps so he could carry most of Barry's weight. They hobbled along together. Kerion was careful not to dislodge the medrob.

They passed an odd sight. Two halves of an autovolt. The autovolt had been bisected as if by a laser, cut in two. Looking closely, they saw that the head had its top cut away. Barry spotted the top of the head under a bench.

"What did this?"

"Whatever it is, I want one," said Kerion.

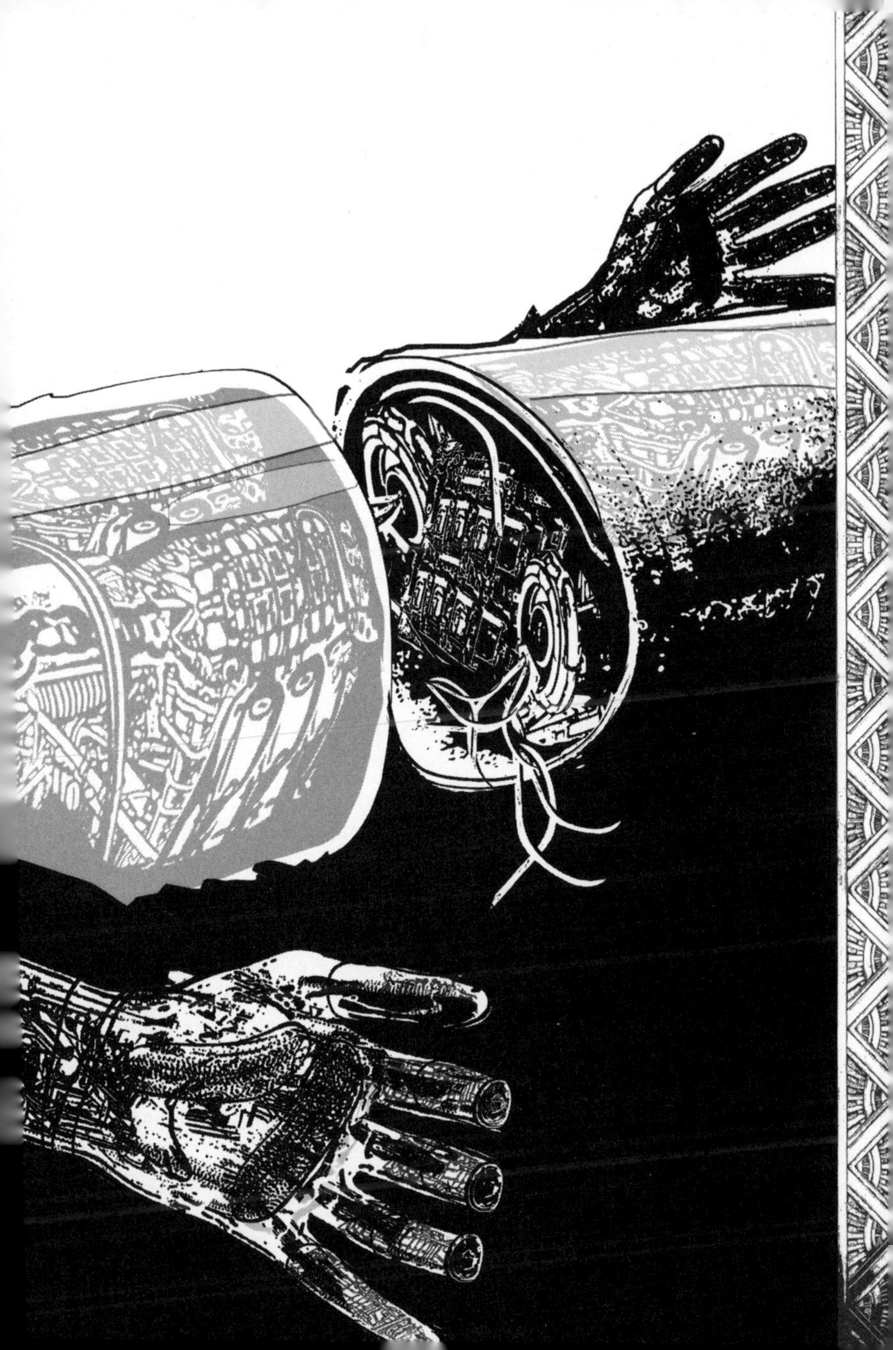

//THEBIRDMAN//

Smiley was standing on a green hill. The grass was tall and swished like water up and down. They were knee-high in the green, totally still. They had on an environment suit with a closed-shell helmet. On the front of the helmet a drippy smiley face had been painted. Smiley had three crows that stood on the broad mantle, and one atop their head.

"Is he real?"

"Yes."

"Are we going to talk to him?"

"I think we should see if they will talk to us."

Just then the crow flew from his head and perched near them.

"What do you want?" it said clearly.

"Can we pass through?" Kerion said to the bird. It looked at him with one eye, then the other, then lighted toward the man, who reached out his arm.

"Is it spliced?" Kerion said looking at Barry

"A My-Mutant maybe? The conservation zones have all sorts of things that Standardization does not allow. After the Third Extinction, there was less snobbery about what counted as worth saving."

The bird flew back.

"No," it said clearly.

Kerion pointed east toward the wall.

Smiley nodded.

Barry and Kerion turned east, away from the hills.

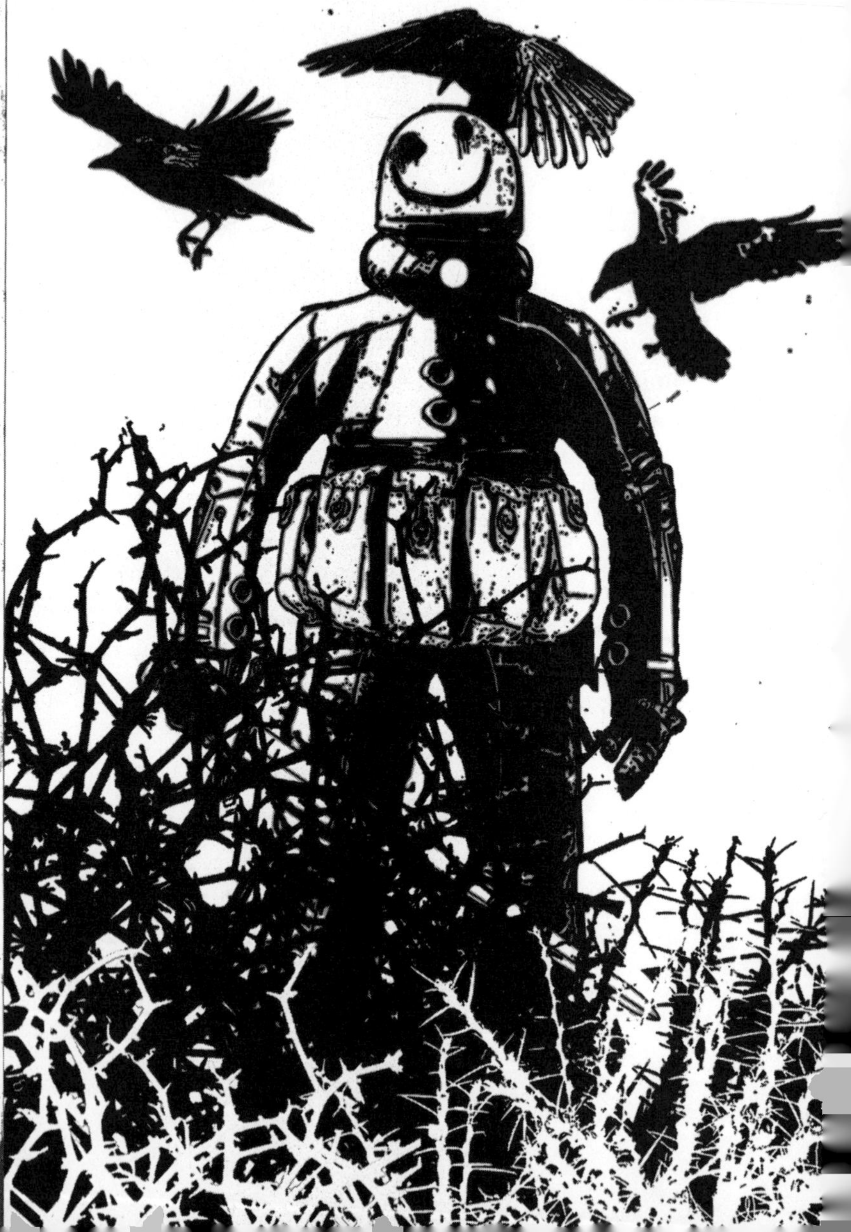

//LEFTORRIGHT//

They walked a long way, nervous of every sound.

They had grown accustomed to the empty streets of the automatic world, but this natural landscape was full of startling things for the alert and ignorant. Every bird and rustling animal might have been an autovolt moving to engage.

They found no corpses. This arrived in their consciousness in its absence. Making them aware of all the things they were used to seeing that they did not.

"Where is everyone?"

"I don't know. Better string that bow."

"It feels very easy for us to be snuck up on here."

"I agree."

Barry found a long branch and used it as a crutch, freeing his father up to watch more carefully, bow at the ready.

"What happened to your hand?"

Kerion had bound his hand tightly. The wound, though painful, reacted properly to the disinfectant coagulant gauze he had applied. He wasn't sure he could accurately use the bow any longer. Barry was too injured to even try.

"I'll tell you later."

They passed through the low parkway and began to climb a hill. The tops of the building peeked up into view again and both Kerion and Barry began to relax. They made their way cautiously but carefully forward.

A three-story-tall fence line ran in a curved kilometer in either direction out of sight.

"Left or right?"

"Left."

They went on until the wall became covered in a tall hedge of thorny brambles which seemed like it might support their weight to climb. Kerion didn't think Barry could make it without help. He wasn't sure he could do it with his injured hand either.

"I'll try it first."

"No need Dad, there's a door over here."

//CONSERVATION//

The door had not been opened automatically or otherwise. It was hinged and had no signs of electric power of any sort. The bramble had begun to grow across it. They pulled away the branches and there was a sign: LEAVING CONSERVATION ZONE—Thank you for your visit. FUNNY LAND supports all green initiatives.

Barry pulled back a handful of leaves from the bars of the gate. He yanked and they did not come, he yanked hard, and the tangle let loose. It was bound to the door, which was not locked, and Barry fell back as the door opened. It hurt, and the medrob clenched tightly to hold on, which hurt more.

Barry looked up and there was an autovolt on the other side of the door.

//TEST//

Barry scrambled backward, kicking to get away.

The sudden fear pulsed through him. He wasn't able to get his breath to warn his dad. Kerion was right there though, dropping in front of his son, the raygun raised.

But the autovolt just stood there.

"I don't get it."

"Shoot it," Barry said.

"Wait."

They both quivered, breathing hard. They had not been this close to a functioning autovolt, only a few meters, without a battle for their lives.

"Is it dead?"

"I can see the focus rings moving. It sees us. Throw a rock at it."

"Dad?"

Kerion had the ray gun up, "If it comes forward, I'll burn it down."

Barry threw a small stone which went "tink" on the clear skin of the autovolt.

"No, something bigger."

Barry found a large rough stone, tipped it backward to free it from the dirt, and marveled at the number of bugs that were revealed. He lifted it with two hands above his head and flung it.

The autovolt stepped aside and backward one stride and the heavy stone landed, rolled where it had been.

"It's functioning. Why isn't it…?"

"They can't come in." Kerion said, then more excitedly, "They can't come in."

Kerion rubbed his face, the beard upended. "We have to test it. Barry, don't let me get too excited about this, we have to test it."

"Test what?"

"The conservation zone keeps them out. It's a foundational protocol, at the beginning, there were, ahhh, *protocols*," he said, pacing, waving his hands as he spoke. "There were reasons we were doing it. A sick planet, so we made the green belts. When we took you to Munson Park when you were two, we had to leave the pod-car, and no one was allowed any autorobs. Why didn't I…"

"What's so special about them?"

"Robots can't go in the green belts. They're natural preserves."

"But what do the autovolts care about preserving any-thing? They killed, they killed *everybody*."

"It answers the question as to where they were made maybe? I think that an old protocol supersedes their imperative. They hunt people yes, but the conservation zone protocol overrides their own program. Ranger Robo was there, but his assistant said..."

Kerion looked at Barry and smiled.

"Why are they listening to that?"

"Everything automatically has to, I guess. It is odd. But it's true..."

Kerion took up his pack and bandolier. "We're going back. We may have just accidentally found and walked through the safest place on Earth."

//LOSS//

"What are we looking for?"

"There."

"What are those? Wait, those are old solar arrays."

"Old style but well-maintained. See those round things? Those are habitats. I think there are lights on."

"Dad?"

"Look, you're sweating, let me look at—Barry—oh you're—"

"Oh, that's a lot of… blood," Barry said, then fell over.

//PEOPLE//

"Just rest."

"I knew it. Look. People. Look at the people!"

"Can we…"

"Well, we have to…"

"But we've got to be careful…"

"Remember what happened in the subway, and on the train…"

"I remember, Barry, but I don't know how to fix you and you need rest and power for the medrob. I…"

//INTENTIONALIZED//

They approached cautiously, the round dwellings looked intact, well used, and well maintained. Not by automatics though. The paint didn't always match, there was stacked wood, and a garden. There were signs of half-finished projects, and robots didn't take breaks.

They came up slowly. Barry had the raygun and was gripping onto Kerion's backpack. Kerion had the bow out and an arrow nocked.

They heard the voice, loud and amplified.

"Be at peace. You are home. Your cares are lifted. You are safe here. Safe Garden welcomes you. The things that others fear cannot reach you here."

A figure strode out into space between the lodgings. She was very tall and hung with all manner of finery. Barry recognized some of it as having come from the museum they had passed.

"Keep your weapons if they make you feel safe, but soon under my blessing you will see you do not need them. I am the Hierophant, keeper of Intention. Welcome travelers, you are safe here."

A line of children came forward and lined up in front of The Hierophant.

"Keep your mask on Barry."

"If it will keep you feeling safe, please do, but we are all fit and healthy. Precautions are important though."

She motioned and people began to emerge from the lodgings. Kids and teens, all adolescents but no adults.

"What is this place?" Barry asked.

"Most of us found this place years ago. But a few, like yourselves, have come seeking the false tower to find instead the promise of our Safe Garden. I built this place before the Fall, certain it was coming. You can give up your journeys and fears. Think no more of them. Welcome."

//SAFEGARDEN//

There were perhaps two hundred people at Safe Garden, trauma victims and survivors of terrible things. But they each took their intentions seriously and took a pill each day that kept their mind clear of difficult thoughts. The Hierophant was their leader and took to the task with reverence that Barry found intoxicating, even though his father forbade him from taking any pills.

"Who fixes these?" Barry asked, looking at their dwellings and gardens.

"We do. No robots here. Which is our wish."

"Which is our wish." Barry heard a few echoes from the crowd.

"Our labor sets us free," the Hierophant continued.

"They've been intentionalized," Kerion said.

"Dad?"

"At Safe Garden, we teach that what you think about, happens. So I tell them not to think about the autovolts so they don't arrive," said the Hierophant.

"Which is absurd."

"And yet you stand in the proof of our miraculous existence," the Hierophant said.

"And when something happens? Something bad?"

"Here we teach that if they don't think about bad things they won't happen," the Hierophant said loudly.

Kerion held her look.

"You teach. You're the only adult here."

"Not so," the Hierophant said.

"It must be difficult to keep them all safe."

She smiled, "Many hands make light work."

The Hierophant stood, her robes unfurling, and said loud enough for others to hear clearly: "You think too often of bad things, so I'm afraid something bad is going to happen to you. If you will learn intentionality, you can stay. If not, you must, for the safety of all here, go on your own path. We will give you food and provisions; we have more than we need."

"Through intention do we make our world," the people of Safe Garden said in unison.

"I just don't know what happened to you that you deny a miraculous thing when you see it."

"It's not a miracle. You live in a Conservation Zone."

"The miracle is that I choose to live here because I believed society was poisoned, that automation was evil, and I was right. We made a safe place for ourselves with our thoughts."

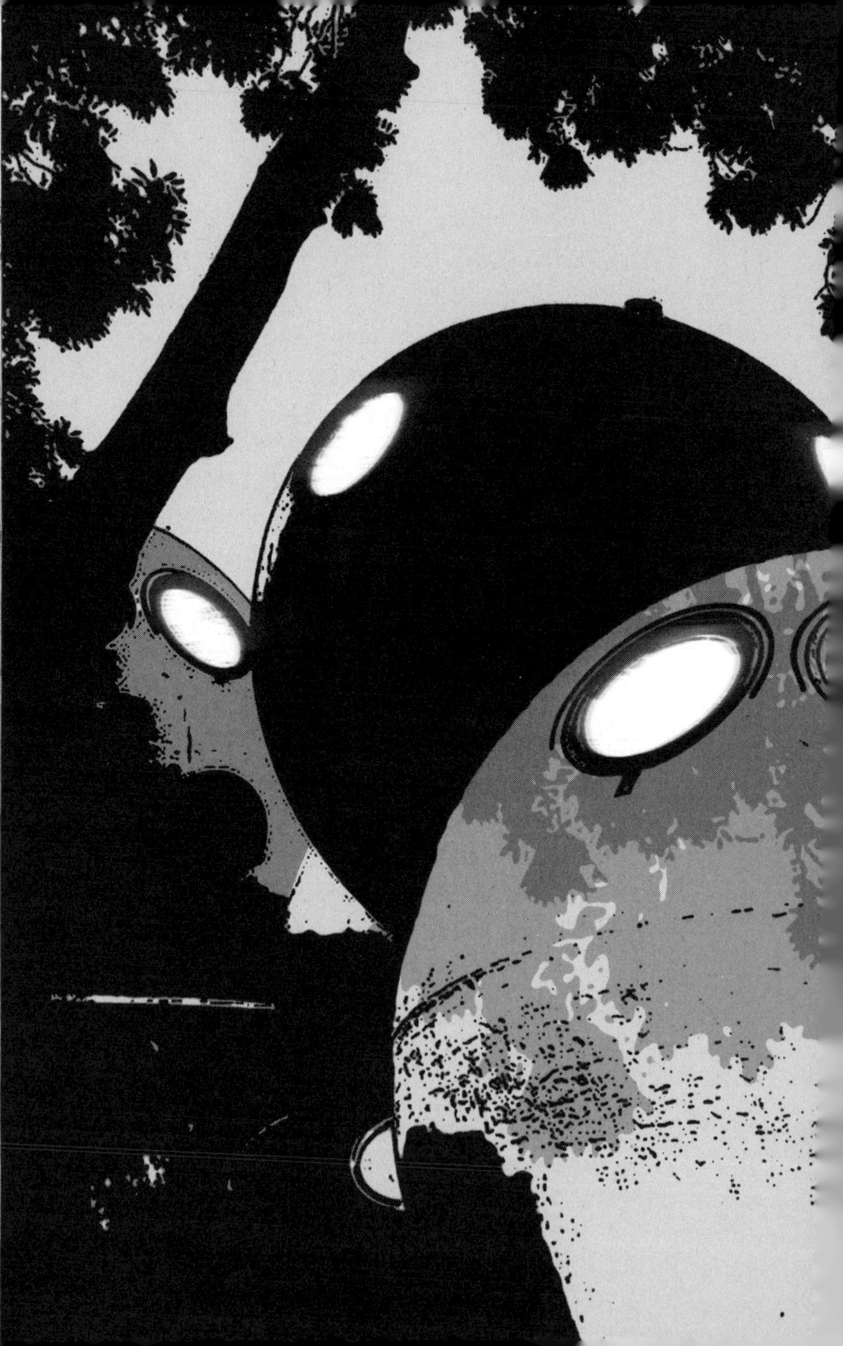

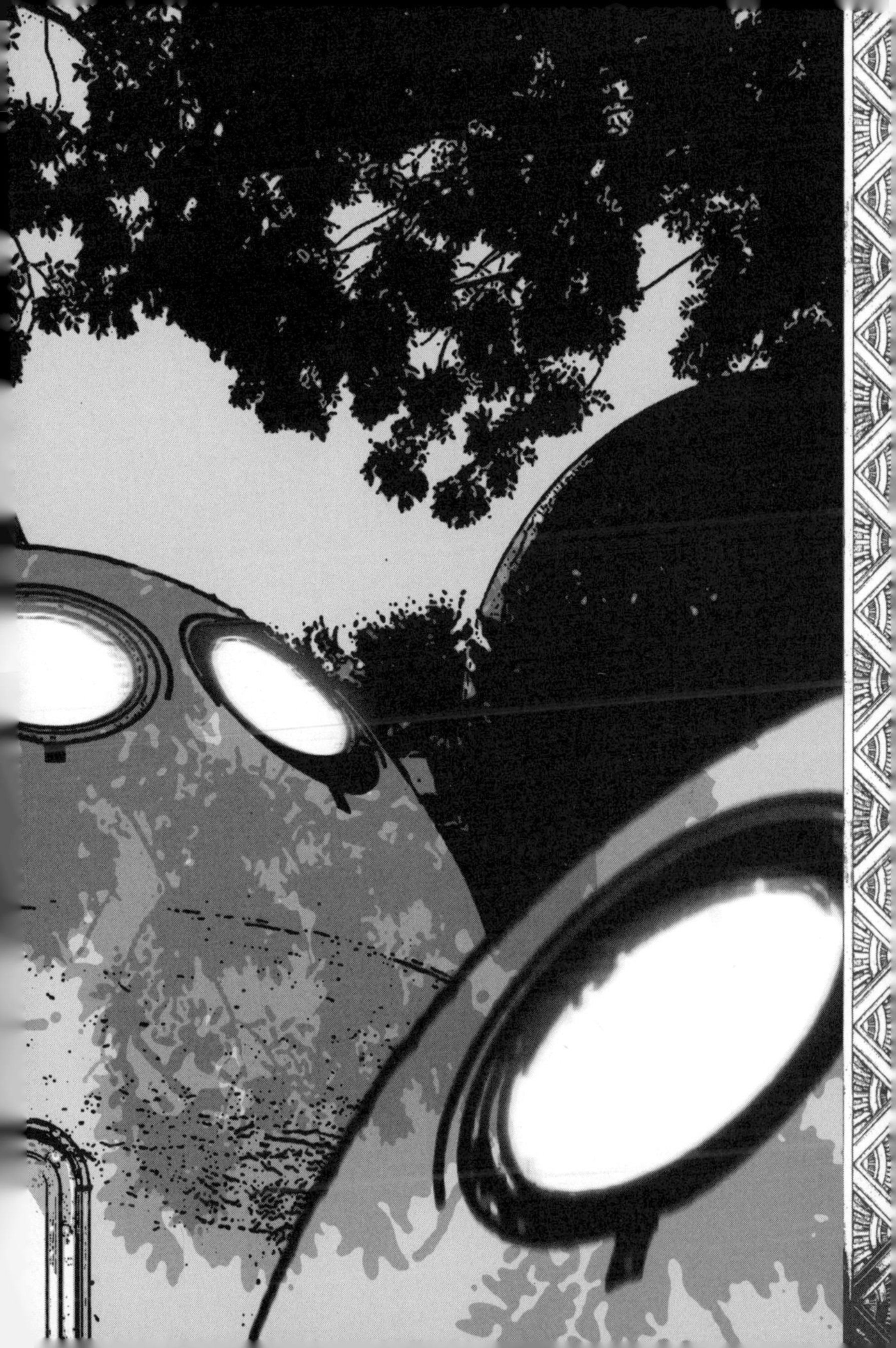

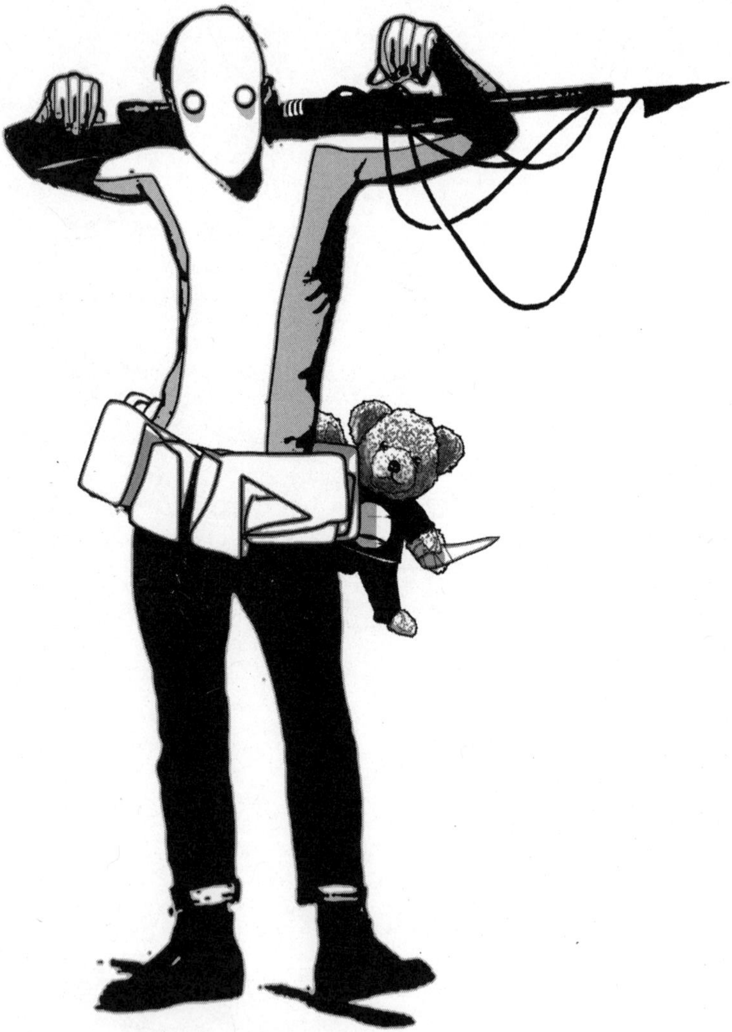

"Society allowed you to live here by choice without persecution, it's by their leave that you are here, not some magical wish. It was a condition of the peace."

"Come now, no need to dwell on the past. Those thoughts will bring back that time. Let's think about the future. Let's believe in a better time and make it thus."

"You're delusional," Kerion said.

"We're safe."

"You're going to get all of these people killed. All of these people who can, from here, look to a real possible future." Kerion pointed toward the tower.

"The elevator is a lie of technology. A tower ready to fall."

"What happened here? You know, don't you?"

"Such thoughts are forbidden. They will bring ruin."

"You need to help these people."

"They are, in fact, safe here. That tower offers chances, not facts. Gamble your life if you want. But the boy is staying here." The Hierophant waved and a tall adolescent stepped forward with bravado, a rifle slung across his shoulders.

"We're leaving."

"Yes, *you* are. The boy will stay here. Safe."

"This isn't a paradise, it's a prison. Leave with us!" Kerion said, pointing to the great machine of the elevator.

"No. The others left. They choose me. I protect them. I protect them from anything that will hurt them."

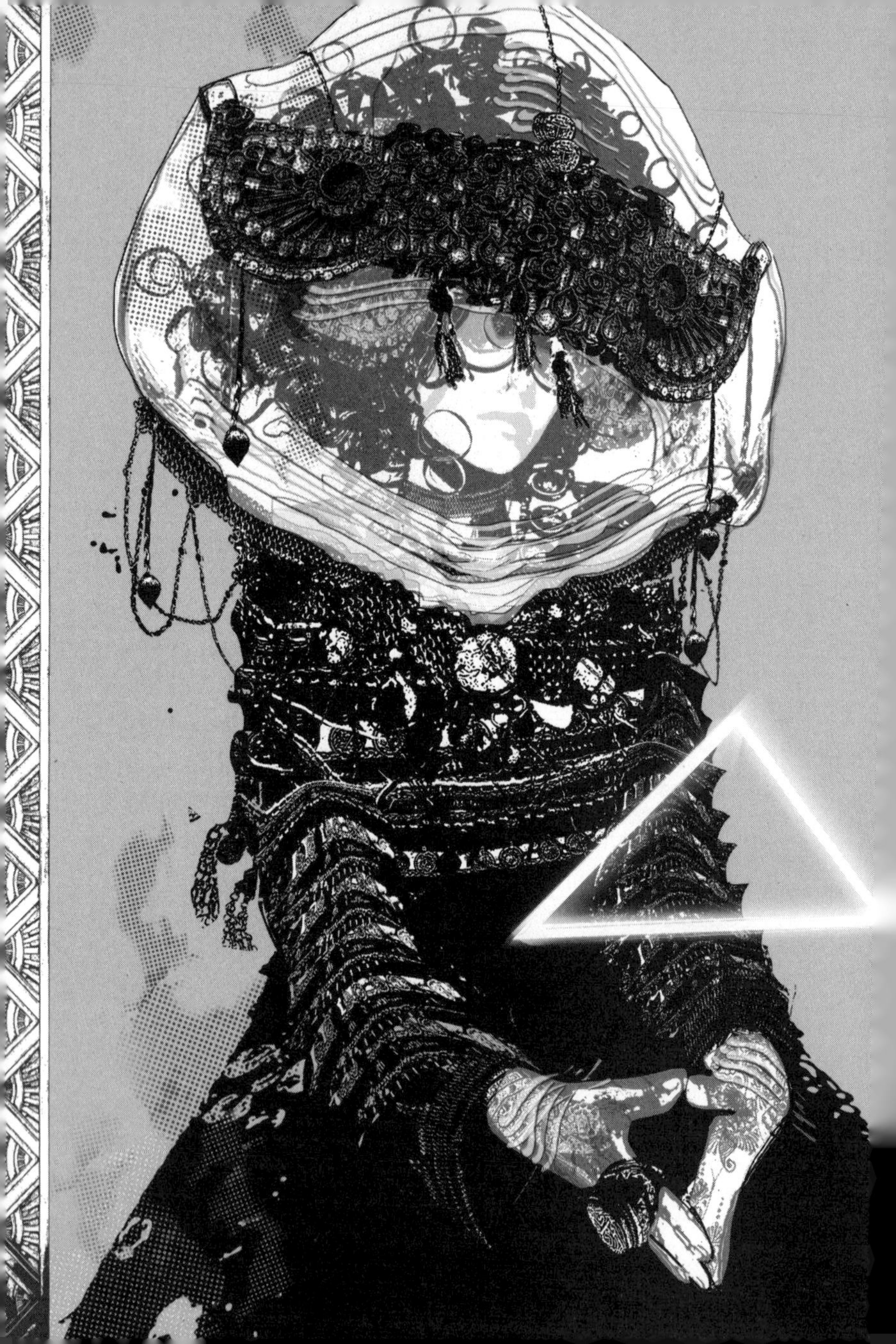

"Even the truth."

"What they believe matters more because it gives them a special place free from harm."

"You don't even believe what you're saying."

"We all believe it."

"Which just happens to make you very important?"

"I am important. So are you. You brought your son to us. Just as I told them someone would. It's time for your intentions," the Hierophant said.

The Bear Boy pointed the rifle at Kerion.

The raygun flashed and the rifle burst into flames. Bear Boy fell backward, unhurt but very confused. Barry had the arrow up, pointed at the Hierophant.

"We've made our intentions clear I think," Barry said.

"This is salvation. You'll be safe here," the Hierophant said.

"Only from the robots," Kerion said.

//CASTLEINTHESKY//

There, without gravity, without the ability to even touch your own skin, clad in the sheaves of armor, flesh trembling as hissing thrust exhales to angle you to apogee, then dive toward the night side of the earth, it's there that you wish it could be anyone, anything else that could do the thing that you must do. Wishing that machines could be smart enough, foolish enough to fight without calculating odds. Knowledge that you are the smart part of a bomb. You curse the waste of a life, of that experience, of that potential.

Then the point defences begin to find you and the heat warnings chime and the cluster bombs begin to go off. XV99, which the insurgents had renamed Heaven, spinning ring stacked on ring, a last castle in the sky.

The 7th war had been about intentions and promises. It had been about things denied, a postmodern reality. A desire for libertarian self-governance and consumerist despotism.

Or had it been about seeing what all those innovations could do, about opening Pandora's box and letting everything out? Like children, each with a box full of toys, lining them up and supposing what would happen if they all fought.

//FLESHANDBLOOD//

Kerion stopped. Looked back.

"Listen to me, I need you to hear me. Out here there are lots of dangerous things. The autovolts, the burning areas, the wild robots, other people. Those are physical dangers, but those aren't in our control. We react to them; we do our best. That's all we can do. But certain ways of thinking are *very* dangerous to us. More dangerous than bullets or raybeams. Autovolts are a system that is built to find us and kill us. That might not be all they are, but that's all they are to us. *They* want you to think you can change things by wishing."

"What if they're right!? What if they made it happen? We SAW THEM planting trees instead of killing. We saw them and you didn't tell them. Why? Because it supports their idea? You're so afraid of being wrong about these people that you didn't tell them."

Kerion felt the cold.

"It's okay to hate me for all of this, but you have to do that before danger starts or when it's over. While things are happening you need to think clearly, and emotion gets in the way of all that. You did good back there, and I'm proud of you."

"Oh, I guess I'm your good little robot!" Barry said it and then tried to suck it back, tried to wish time backward, but it was done.

"I'm your father, Barry, despite it all, and I'm going to do what I can to keep you safe until I can't anymore." Kerion hung his head. "Then you'll have to do it yourself."

"They are all kids. All kids like me."

"I wish that were true, but it doesn't make it so."

//OLD SHOES//

Walking down through the dunes, amid the swaying speargrass, father and son.

Barry stumbled in the deepening ruts of the shifting grains, and Kerion took his hand to steady him. Kerion did not let go, and Barry did not pull away and they walked hand in hand toward the tangle of vines that was the conservation wall on the horizon.

Half buried along the path was a pair of old shoes, laces knotted together.

//BIGDIFFERENCE//

"Well, what do you think?"

"I can see three—no—five of them."

"That's a big difference."

"It's five."

"Okay. Now what?"

"Those three on the street there aren't our concern, unless the closest one signals them."

"How do we prevent that?" Kerion asked.

"You—You are going to move around to the automat and put a coin in. When it activates and they see you, the closest will investigate. Once those close to us stand down, there is no reason for the far ones to investigate. Then you're going to do your zap trick. And while that's happening, I'm going to enter through the side door."

"What if there's one in there that you can't see?"

"There isn't."

"You sound sure."

"I'm sure," Barry said.

"Then that's our plan," Kerion said.

//THEWHEELKEEPSON//

"The whole base of the tower is an amusement park."

The place was a Funny Landing, the biggest entertainment cartoon-themed world of the century. A strange welcome to the world if you came down the elevator, a playful farewell if you were going up. All of it ringed by a tended garden reclaimed from the wasteland.

"Arrivals and departures celebrating the journey."

"Or maybe just being asked to forget how dangerous a place space can be."

"That too, maybe. But you know people have been up there a long time. Once the Lunar treaties were signed, and the Venus Accord, the population 'problem' sort of started solving itself."

"Well, it's solved now," Barry said looking out over the empty boardwalks, thousand-metre Ferris wheel, Spinning Teacups, Gravity Shoes, Spin Flux, The Loop, and Tunnel of Love.

Only a few years ago this would have been a marvel. But now, amusements did not seem to be a thing to build acres of structures for.

"Everything is on."

"True."

"It looks so strange, all of it just whirling there."

"Yeah."

"I see one thing that's really good about it."

The coaster arrived, finishing its journey, unlocking all the doors and restraints. Beckoning.

"What?"

"No lines," Barry said.

"True," Kerion said with a growing smile. "How are you feeling?"

The medrob had detached two days ago, leaving a very tender collection of slowly dissolving stitches. It had assumed a graying, curled shape like a dead pill bug, displaying 'zero efficiency,' then nothing at all.

They didn't say out loud what they would do. In a way they needed to keep it a secret for that moment. An agreed-upon deceit of safety.

"Welcome aboard!"

They laughed

The autovolt came around the cotton candy stand.

They were still laughing.

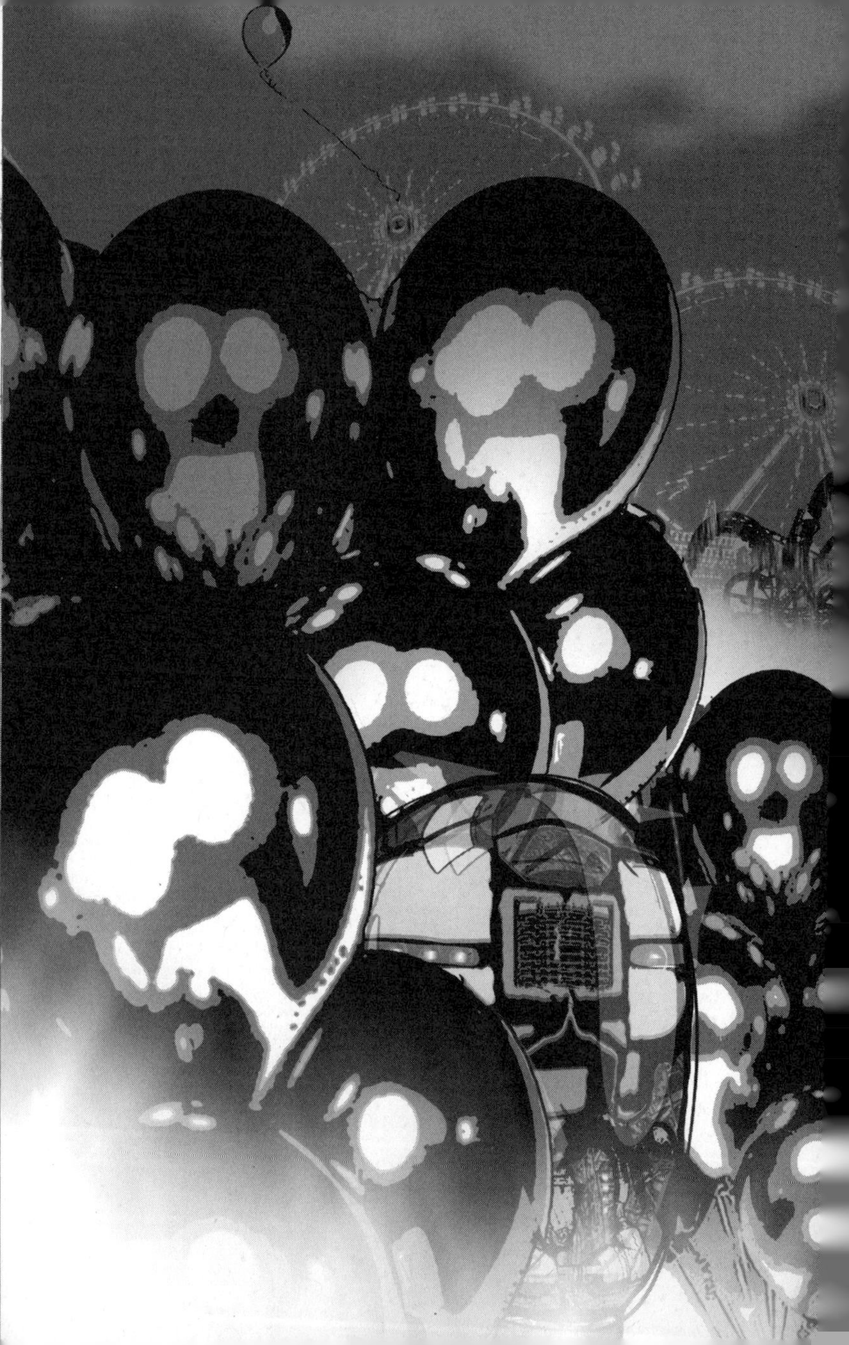

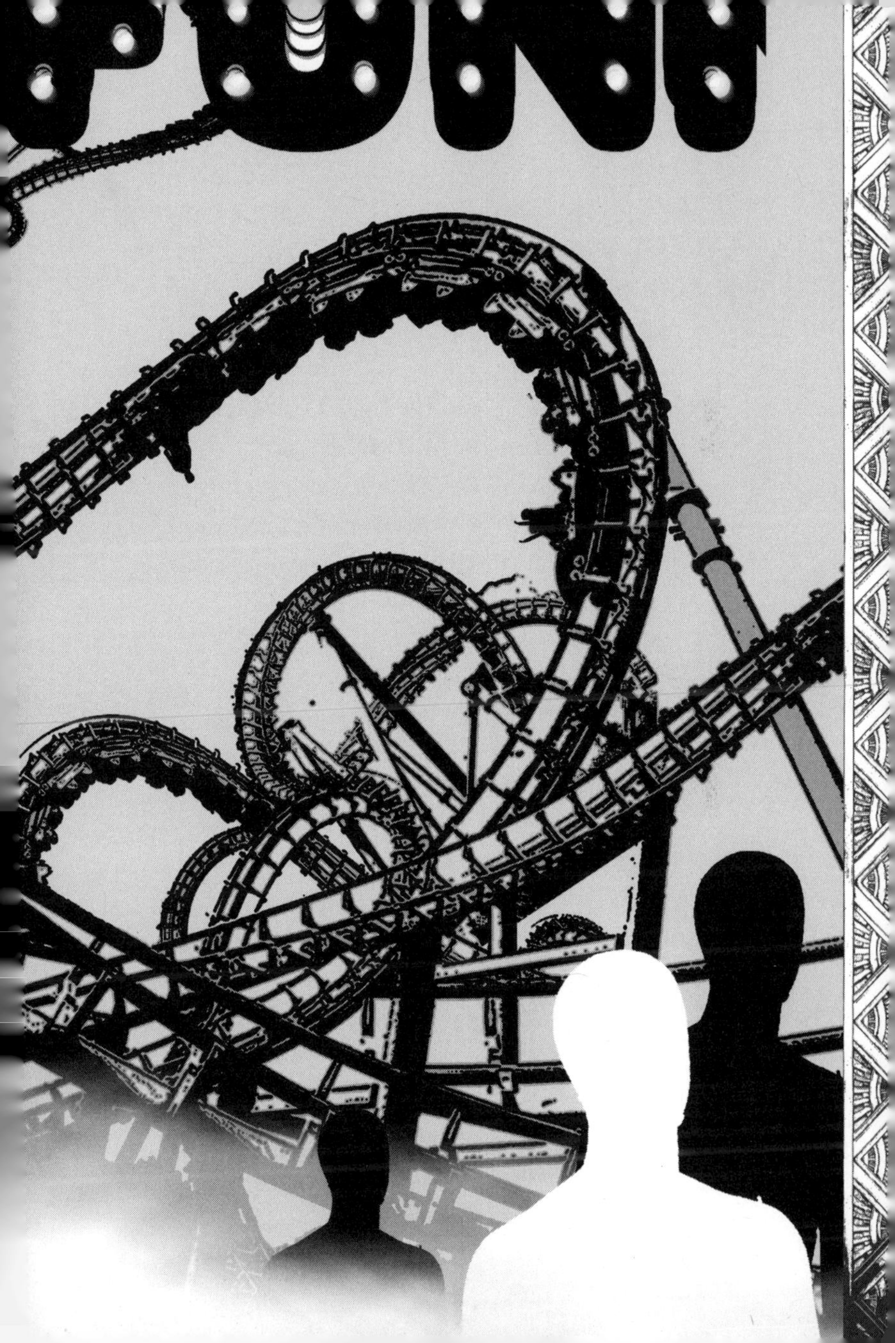

They looked at each other, still laughing, then jumped onto the roller coaster together. They boarded the first carousel. It had an open canopy and an old-fashioned click-in seat belt harness. Nothing that could autolock or seal. The carousel swept away and at once the exhilaration rose in them as they rose into the air. They clutched each other's hands, squeezing as they swept up into the sky. When the ride was over, the coaster came sliding down the long slope toward the waiting autovolt. Breathing hard from the laughing and yelling, they both cut their restraints while the cars were still moving.

The autovolt strode forward.

"I am unit 8347-34," Kerion said.

Barry remained very still, trying not to laugh.

//STUPIDMOUSE//

"When we got on that last rail train, I thought I'd bring you here."

"Because you think I'm still that kid."

"Because I wanted you to remember *being a kid*. I felt like a kid again the first time I saw the Backbone. It was right after the fight in dining car and we were talking about that stupid mouse, and I thought about the time we went to a Funny Landing near home, and I remembered how you'd played robot tag in the Zap Pit with that oversized mouse."

"I remember that. It was fun. The Zap Pit, not the train."

"You would duck out of bounds—it couldn't leave the play area—then you ran around to the side and jumped back in, then out again when it started moving."

"You thought of that because of the autovolts, how they were acting back there."

Kerion was very still for a moment, sweat on his palms and back, a realization.

"Barry, we have to go and look at something."

"Dad?"

But Kerion was moving, rubbing his head, light in his eyes.

"Come on!"

//CONSERVE//

The Ferris wheel took them ten stories up before they could see what they needed to see. They rode it round three times, each time using the portable Sight Seer to zoom in on the rise of the wheel and to review the recording on the drop.

"Many hands make light work," Kerion said. "She knew, Barry. She knew. 'Many hands make light work.' She knows it's borrowed time."

"Dad, I don't understand. What are we doing?"

"It's a conservation zone," Kerion said.

"I know, you said, we saw, but what do you mean?"

"That swarm we saw. The autovolts are taking part of the city apart to balance the books. They are planting trees and wilding the area so that they can clear Safe Garden off the map. It is what they did. Oh, I understand now. This space is next to the amusement park. The park could only be built if a conservation zone was maintained to balance the environmental impact. Look!"

"Dad, we have to do something."

"I don't know what—"

"We've got to warn them—" Barry said, looking over the carousel anxiously.

//THELINE//

The autovolts were there. A hundred of them at least. They were all standing in a single file line. The line stretched from the park gate back along the street to the moving sidewalk. And there was another one, carried by the sidewalk. Just as it seemed it would bump into the line of the others, the whole procession took a single unified step forward and the autovolt from the sidewalk took its place at the back of the line. At the front of the line, a single autovolt walked into the park down the pathway and through the gate they had themselves come through.

Kerion motioned for Barry to lower and they did, very slowly, back behind the roof peak of the ICE CREAM DREAM they had climbed up on for a better vantage.

They heard the zzzz zzzz zzzz of the autovolt's passage getting fainter as it went past them in the direction of the hills

"Every tree they plant moves the conservation zone back. They aren't extending it. They are moving it. They can't change the protocol, so they are following the rules. That's what machines do. They follow rules."

"It's happening. They've moved the conservation zone. I think this is the force that is going to…"

"We didn't try hard enough. To make them come out of there."

"To change their minds?"

"Yeah. All those kids. Do you think we tried?"

Kerion was unable to lie. "No. I don't think we did."

"They're going to die. All of them?"

"A few, might, like us, find a way…"

"So we have to carry it, I guess." Barry hung his head, breathing deeply. Shaking.

"As far as we can," Kerion said.

Maybe there is a way to help them, Barry thought. *Maybe there is a way.*

"The new zone!" he said. "The new zone, we have to get there. I know where it is. From there we can…"

//DONOTLOOK//

They had found a place where a fallen tower rested on the top of the conservation wall. They had moved up the slanted improvised lookout and taken cover.

It was a good idea, but it was too late. The autovolts were doing their ruthless, careful work. Dispassionately removing the people of Safe Garden.

"I'm sorry son, but I cannot let you look. If I see a way to help, if there is a way to help, I promise you, we will. But I can't let you look before I do."

They could hear that it was bad.

Kerion knew that Barry shouldn't see.

"Give me the Sight Seer and keep your head down."

Kerion had seen war and participated in it. There was a desperation that overcame both sides as the will to live came on like a tide. With the lifeless autovolts there was only a careful, measured protocol. They did not care about being injured when pressed and did not act without a strong margin for success. Safe Garden had not had to face them. If the

Hierophant could be believed, many were survivors who had fled there on The Last Christmas. From horror to reprieve, then told to forget. Forgetting is not a useful solution to an ongoing problem: it grants that problem the ability to surprise again. The people of Safe Garden had clearly been surprised. No amount of wishing would help them now.

"Dad!?"

"I'm looking. Stay there."

The Safe Garden folks had gathered around the Hierophant. Protecting her with their own fragile bodies. In the group of busy, organized autovolts, one was moving strangely. It moved carefully and differently amid the chaos. There was blood and resistance and people all around, autovolts moving in pursuit, and one autovolt that seemed to pick its way from place to place. When they saw it was carrying the arrow that Barry had used, they understood the path it was following.

"Slippery is back."

Slippery stopped in front of one autovolt, then another, then another. Each time they stopped the thing they were doing to fall into step with Slippery.

"I want to see."

"No."

At that instant, there was a voice. Someone had crept up behind them. Barry turned, knife out. Kerion threw himself between his son and the voice.

"Come with me," the crow said, then hopped twice and flew away. At the bottom of the fallen tower they saw Smiley. Smiley waved, then waved them off and ran. An autovolt followed Smiley soon after. Another autovolt stopped where Smiley had been, turned, saw them, and began climbing.

//SMILE//

They jumped from the leaning tower to the top of the conservation wall, which had a treed walkway atop it. Then they scrambled under the crumbling overhang of the building, up into the smashed wall and half ran and half slid down the tube shaft of the interior elevator.

"Is it following?"

"Assume it is."

They exited the building through the upturned remains of its once grand entryway. They slid down a great bronze statue of Villi De Mandir, First Lady of Solar Glass, and out into the street.

Barry was breathing hard and hurting. Kerion stopped their progress to check and make sure the stitches had held.

There in the street was Slippery and his cadre of autovolts, coming forward at a steady jog.

"Barry."

But Barry was ready and loosed an arrow using the autosight, which struck the right autovolt in the leg, the arrow piercing the clear shell, slowing it.

"Last one then we run," Barry said, sighting in on Slippery and reading the rangefinder on the autosight.

Barry let the arrow fly and Slippery reached over and pulled Lefty in front of the shot. The arrow pierced the shell and sparked on the inside.

"Did you see that?"

"We've got to—"

"Oh, Polish is there, and maybe Rattle and..."

"You think Slippery gathered up a few with a grudge?"

"No, but a few with experience against us."

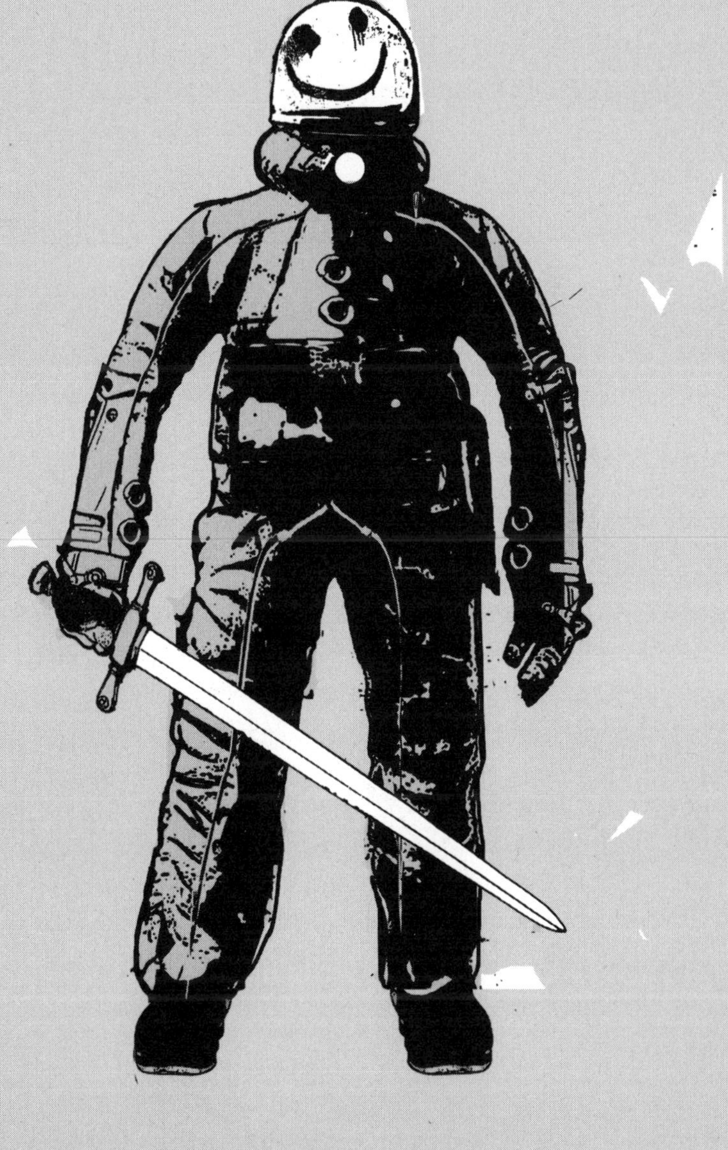

//BONES//

"Dad, I think that's where they want us to go."

"In here. Oh, no."

They were in some sort of inventory space. There were no other doors.

"Up there?"

There was a maintenance or ventilation grill in the ceiling.

"Climb the shelves."

Cans and bottles and boxes fell as they climbed.

The door opened.

Polish came in.

Polish didn't climb after them.

It turned back to the door and sealed it.

It looked at them and then pointed the nozzle on the arm at them. The tiny opening hissed and sputtered. Greenish yellow vapor launched forward feebly then arched in a fan and began to collect on the floor.

"Lucky," Barry said. He had his knife working at the edges of the grill. Kerion could see that they were not going to fit.

The autovolt remained motionless. The gas churned, rolling around the lowest shelf, then rising, the volume growing as the autovolt's mounted tank kept releasing it into the chamber.

Kerion knew that soon they would fall from the shelves, maybe as bones, then be gone.

The door chimed.

There was an odd noise.

The autovolt's head and arms clattered to the floor. It tried to turn around, then its torso slid away to the floor and the legs toppled over. The top of the door fell into the room. Barry and Kerion looked at each other, frozen for a moment at this impossible thing.

Someone reached over the missing top of the door, unlatched it, and stepped into the room. They moved like a human and wore an environment suit that had a dome helmet with a smiling face crudely painted on the front.

Smiley held a long, pointed sword in one gloved hand. At their feet, the vapor swirled but was receding, flowing out from the room. That crude smiley face looked up, then down, then up again.

"Okay. Come down," they said in a very muffled voice.

//SOSMOOTH//

Smiley pushed the point of the sword into the floor and the weapon stuck there. Then the stranger lifted their hands to grasp each side of the smiley face. The helmet turned with a click.

She was older than Barry's mom had been, and this woman had brown skin and lots of white hair, perfectly white, not from age though, at least Barry didn't think so, because her face was so smooth. Barry kept looking back at that drippy painted face on the front of the helmet.

"Some of them say it's creepy, but, well, my son painted it on when I said we'd go to Happy Landing." She traced the painted smile with her thumb in a way that made Barry sure he shouldn't ask where her son was.

"Thank you for the help." Kerion said.

"Do you know the way out of here?" Barry asked.

"You can come with me but—"

"But what?"

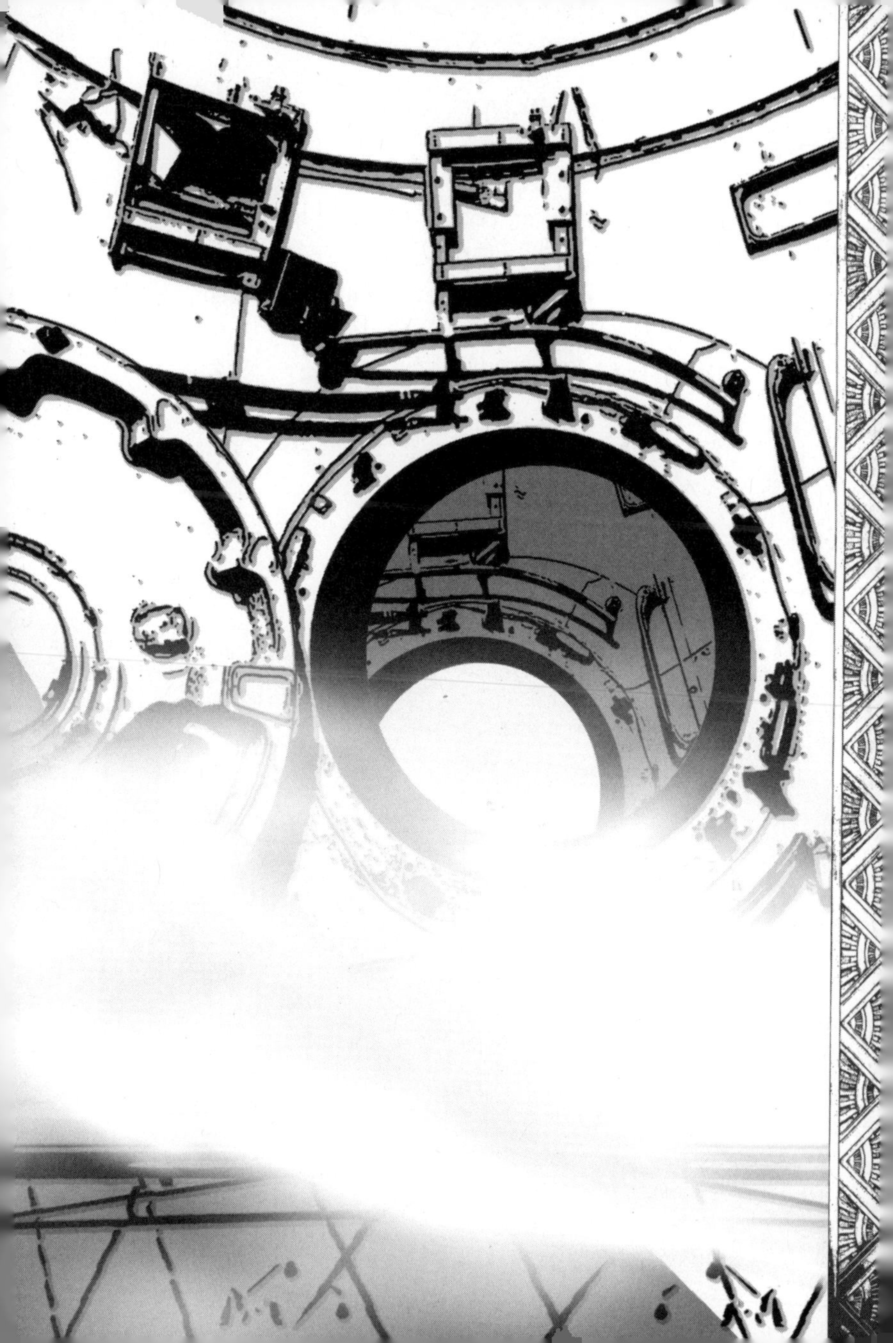

"Nothing, you *can* come with me, but, well, this is awkward."

Kerion looked at the severed autovolt and the sword standing upright out of the floor.

"I was hoping I could come with *you*."

//CEILINGOFRAINBOWS//

Crows flapped around making enormous noise. One of them lighted on Smiley's shoulder and said, "We've got to go if we're going."

They headed through a long balloon-filled space. A hundred thousand balloons made a ceiling of rainbows.

As she walked, Barry could swear he could see the shape of her moving legs through the sword.

"Is your sword made of glass?"

"Yes. It was made as a silly prototype, a media prop. Do you remember the Clever Knight commercials?"

"What are commercials?"

"Ways to make you buy things and have interest in a product to buy," Kerion said.

"Betweeners. Sure. We don't do that on Earth anymore you said."

She knelt and looked at Barry, smiling.

"Well, not all the worlds up there are automatic ones. So we had lots of commercials. Well, there was a commercial where they let people on the street cut through stuff. Everyone thought it was fake at first. Random folks cutting through pipes and old rockets. It was a low-energy way to replace lasers or something manufactured on orbital mining stations."

"It was a lie though, wasn't it?"

"The low energy cost part was. A huge upfront cost in energy to produce tools with this material, so it didn't catch on. Great commercial though. I loved it as a kid. This," she said, pointing to the weapon, "is that sword from the commercial. It was in the Camelot Collection here. But it works, the technology is amazing. Stacked up molecules in such a way to make it very strong and very, very sharp."

She held the tip over the concrete barrier.

"Watch."

She let it go. The sword slipped into the concrete right up the hilt with a click. The blade just seemed to disappear.

"Woah," said Barry

"Woah," said Kerion.

"Pull it up," she said. "Careful not to touch anything but the handle."

Barry looked at his dad, Kerion nodded.

Barry stepped forward and took the sword by the hilt. He looked back at Smiley.

"Pull it straight up."

Barry did, and up it went with a slight friction he could feel in the handle. Like the feeling his own knife had on the whetstone.

"The autovolts are just as easy to cut, but I usually can't get close."

"We can," said Barry.

"I know. It's why I've been following you. How do you do that?"

"Prosthetic chassis. I'm automatic from the abdomen down," Kerion reached for his cables and drew one out. "I tell them I'm one of them and when they ask me to prove it, I fry them with my battery reserve."

"Wow."

"It's great," said Barry.

"And you? What's your story?"

"I guess I survived long enough not to be scared by what they are anymore."

"You two are extraordinary."

"What do you want? No stories and no compliments, just say it." Kerion said.

She pointed to the Backbone of Night.

"I want to go back, and I need you to help me get there."

//HEAVYEND//

When they started to make their way toward the Backbone there was a vending machine lying in their path. The automatic snack machine was crumpled from a three- story fall, its contents everywhere.

"What happened?"

Kerion looked up, squinting, "Maybe it happened during the retreat?"

"Greens are fresh."

"Maybe it pushed through a railing, or maybe the railing was being repaired and it wandered through."

"Its legs are still moving."

"The front casing is cracked, let's turn it over. This looks recent, so let's be quick."

"It's heavy," Barry said.

Smiley moved to help but Kerion caught her eye, scowled, and she took up a watch position.

"I'll lift this end," Kerion said. "One, two, *three*."

They gathered fizzy waters and some kelp bars and slices of fresh cucumber.

//NOPE//

"Aren't you guys gonna come with us?" Smiley said to the crows.

They fluttered and hopped back and forth at the threshold to the next area. One of the crows was seesawing its body up and down while balancing on the bust of Mystery Moose. They had come to the Funny Landing Cartoon Caricature Bust Printing area. The high walls were lined with 3D printed cartoon caricatures of tens of thousands of patrons.

"Nope," the crow said at last. Then they all flew off.

"Nope, Nope, Nope, Nope, Nope."

//HEAVYEND2//

There was a vending machine lying in their path, crumpled from a fall, its contents everywhere. Like the last one its legs were struggling to get up. Smiley drew the sword and Kerion looked back the way they had come.

"Lucky?"

"Yeah right."

They took cover behind a token dispenser and looked around.

"Slippery?"

"I thought he was behind us?"

"Okay, so if Slippery is behind us who did this?"

"A protocol? If they predict we visit damaged vending machines, they'll start to damage them and see if we show up."

"But we did. And here we are again. So if it's a trap it's a bad one."

"Learning new things isn't easy."

"Let's double back and take a longer route to the Tower."

//BREADCRUMBS//

"There."

They were up high, something they didn't like to do. But they need to see as much of the space around them as they could. Barry was using the Sight Seer. He passed it to his father.

"Follow the tree line, then go left at the—"

"I see it."

There was an autovolt. It was following their exact path. Well, not exactly, but it was moving from light pole to light pole.

"Oh no." Kerion said.

"What?"

"We've been moving around by day."

"Yeah."

"We didn't notice the light posts were on a motion sensor."

"Oh, no," Barry said. "Like a trail of breadcrumbs."

"We've got to move."

"Just a second." Barry said. He was reviewing the Sight Seer recording. Looking at their recent views. Click.

"Magnify," Barry said. "Magnify," he said again. "Okay, so Slippery *is* following us."

"You're kidding," Kerion said.

"Look at the stains and that canister, it's him alright."

//SLIP//

"Slippery's there again."

"I see him."

"Do you think he's *different*?"

"There *is* something about that chassis. A *slight* variation. And he's clearly curious about something."

"There!" Barry pointed.

"What?"

"That's the bin where we put our wrappers once we got the Sugar Shells."

Kerion felt that warm creep from his stomach to the back of his head.

"I don't know, it could be a coincidence. We've never seen…"

Slippery pushed up the flap and reached inside. He pulled out a crumpled Sugar Shell wrapper. Slippery smoothed it on one palm, turned it over once, then put it back.

"It's investigating. Following clues instead of search grid protocols."

"That's not good," Barry said.

"Yeah," Kerion said, "it sure isn't."

//DELIBERATELYDO//

"Hmmph," Kerion said.

"So we're leaving now."

"Well, yes, but also no."

"You don't think we can outrun him, and we can't outsmart him at the task he's been made to do."

"Exactly."

"So we need to deliberately do something he was not designed to be prepared to handle so we will have an advantage."

Kerion looked at Barry with a smirk of pride then said, "Any ideas?"

"We lead him somewhere we've already been and set a trap," Smiley said.

Kerion frowned.

"What?"

Kerion was quiet, waiting for Barry to consider.

"Okay, right," Barry said. "Since it's been following us for a while and we didn't know it, if we suddenly change our behavior, it'll know we know it's there."

Kerion raised his eyebrows and smiled slightly, then tilted his head, expectantly.

"So then we keep going and don't panic and wait for the opportunity that we don't know about that's likely up ahead…"

//MEEITHER//

They came to a high vantage overlooking a cantilevered balcony system of swimming pools. Each of the pools connected to the one beneath it in J-shaped tubes of water. You could swim between the pools. At the bottom of one pool was a cluster of people, each wearing a weighed belt, each still wearing the recreational breathing apparatus. They had been able to stay hidden a hour perhaps before the air ran out.

From where Smiley, Barry, and Kerion were, they could see three ways down and three ways up. All of them clear. They filled their canteens from a freshwater hydro feature and took a moment to rest.

Barry kept his distance.

"Kid's angry at you."

"I know," Kerion said. "Something about what I said back there really bothered him. We'll work it out."

"I was afraid you'd say something like 'We've got bigger things to worry about.'"

"Never. We will work it out. We're all we've got. I'm just gonna give him a bit of space."

"Listen, I'll keep a lookout and you go look at that, okay?"

"He's fine. He just needs…"

"I know you and I aren't—I know you don't owe me anything. But could you talk to him. Set it right. I just—"

"You've got some things you wish you said, and you didn't?"

"Right. So just—"

"Okay."

Kerion signaled Barry, making a small loop in the air with the two remaining fingers of his hurt hand.

Barry took a deep shaky breath and came over.

"Talk to me," Kerion said.

"It's just that Slippery is gonna be there now, and I won't be able to sleep, and when I eat it's gonna feel weird, like every bite might leave a clue somehow."

"There's something else."

"Yeah well, I'm just supposed to *believe* that there is something out there to help us. I'm just supposed to *believe* that there are more people out there. I'm just supposed to *believe* what you tell me."

"Barry."

"Hey, it's fine. Whatever you *believe*."

"It's hope, Barry. It's different from magic."

Barry sighed and looked away.

"There are a lot of things that can go wrong for us. But a lot of things have gone right for us too. So I hope our plan works, but I don't tell you what I'm worried about because I don't want it to be something else you have to carry. I hope it will work, but I know it might not. I know that any day could be our last one together."

"So you lie to me so I keep *believing* in *you*."

Kerion sighed. "Yes. I don't say that chances are the autovolt will methodically follow us until we're the ones that make a mistake and then it'll kill us. Because that is the likely outcome here. I don't say that I lie awake wondering if I'd rather go first because I don't think I could handle watching it kill you. I don't say that I tell myself however it happens won't matter because then all of this fear and loneliness and doubt will be over for you."

"I don't want to die, Dad."

"Me either, but I don't want to live without you."

"Me either."

Kerion swallowed hard.

"But that's the likely outcome here, and I'm sure it won't be long."

"Hey, Dad."

"Yeah," Kerion said, pulling his son against him.

"Thanks for telling the truth."

"It's heavy but I'll carry this end," Kerion said.

//DANGERDUCK//

The repair robots had not come here. It was a frightening tableau of the horror they had survived. Bodies, diminished by time and scavengers, burned and melted kiosks, fallen autovolts, shattered, their pieces scattered across the scorched floor.

Someone *had* made a last stand here.

"What are these?"

Danger Duck and Mega Mouse and Acro-Bat were all there, standing in silent reverence around a single collection of remains that hunched in an automatic wheelchair. It was a medical model, very advanced. In the hands, a curled collection of pencil and ink drawings.

"What's he got?"

"Early versions of Danger Duck and Mega Mouse and the rest?"

It all made sense at once.

"This was Filbert Wallace."

"The guy who created Happy Landing? I thought he was in cryostasis?"

"He had all his animatronics try to hold the autovolts out of the park. He held them all off while anyone that could, escaped up the tower. The Conservation Zone isn't a ring, this bridge goes over. A last stand."

"Why is he here?"

"They were probably programmed to protect him, so he had to be in danger for it to work."

"Did it work?"

"It seems to have, it would have bought time, but we can't really know. We need to be careful here."

"No five coupon rides?"

"You know what I mean."

//CAROUSEL//

"Look there, and there, those are carousels," Smiley said. "They are like autocars, only as big as a house, and people could fill them up with things they'd need for up there. They move along the track until they are in position, then they become the elevator cars, sealed and safe, since you're rising above the atmosphere. Rising up into…"

"How do we get into one?"

"That's what I'm trying to figure out, what I'd hoped you'd know."

"Well, if they're automatic—"

"That's just it, I don't think they are anymore. This was a last stand; they couldn't leave it to chance that it was compromised. They would have had to switch the control system to manual, maybe lock it somehow?"

"Look at all of them. There must be a hundred. How can we figure out which one is going next?"

"That's what Slippery wants to figure out too."

"Remember that pneumatube line? Their messages weren't getting through, so they came themselves."

"We can't know that," Kerion said.

"What would you do?" Barry asked.

"Okay, so they came down to try and find others, how did they miss the Garden?"

"They would have had to go over the garden with those heavy shells, or maybe they did go in on foot. But the facts we have, the only clue, is right here."

Barry dug in his pack and pulled up the cube.

"Karta," Barry said.

"Map," Smiley said.

"It needs a military grade shell to operate."

"I know a place," Smiley said. "We'll go back tomorrow."

//TROPICALBEACH//

"Full charge, full stomachs, full packs." Barry said.

"I think we need a night off," Kerion said. "Tropical Beach or Lazy River?"

He flipped the switch.

"Beach," Barry said, then looked at Smiley.

"Beach sounds lovely," she said.

The wall became a beautiful beach with a growing sunset, birds calling, a ship sailing in the distance, lapping water.

Smiley went over to the controls and the ceiling became the stars, an incredulous juxtaposition, sun setting on one wall, night sky twinkling above.

"This is 'scoped, live feed from partway up the tower above the clouds." It was a black carpet set with jewels.

"Do you know how to get up there?" Kerion asked.

"Yes," Smiley pointed, "but there is something else very important. Look. There, right there. Did you see that?"

"That moving star? A satellite? Oh, there's another one."

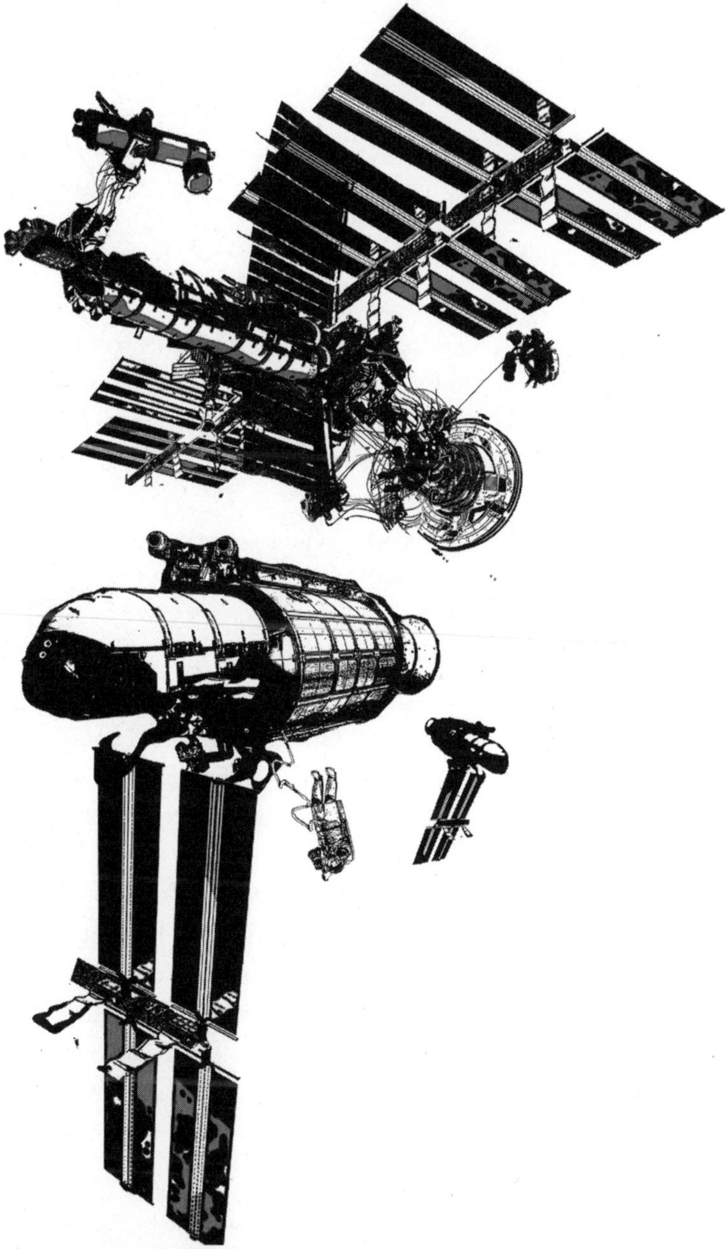

"Ships, Barry, ships on the Crown and maybe beyond."

"It's not a promise, but it's real, and we can see it and we can go there."

"You remind me of my dad."

"You remind me of my son."

"We can live," Kerion said. "We can live. I promise you a life." Kerion slid from the booth, stood and turned, gripping the table with two hands and leaning forward. "Not this false living. Not this pretend thing. A real life. With other people, with more…"

"It's okay, Dad," Barry said. "As long as we are together."

"I love you too. But you'll feel it soon enough. You already said it to me. Survival isn't living, it's the path to living. It's enough for now. But we can do better."

Barry had a sudden insight then, "Until now I thought you learned that from the war, but you didn't, did you?"

Kerion took up the packs, handed one to Smiley and then paused. "No," he said, "from your mother and from you."

Barry stepped forward and hugged his dad around the middle. Squeezing, crying into his shirt. The edge of his father's metal chassis bit into him, but he didn't let go.

Birds chirped and the surf rolled and an artificial sunset cast them both in a golden red glow of a recorded yesterday.

//HURT TO LIE//

They had decided on their next destination, but Smiley had been playfully cryptic about it. She had gone to the corridor to make sure the coast was clear.

Barry had found a maintenance panel under the cushions of the bench seat. He had opened it up and was looking for anything of use.

"Dad!" Barry said, his head and hands still inside the bench seat cavity. The Holographics in the room suddenly flickered and dimmed. Barry withdrew with a huge smile on his face. He had a casing in his hands, about the size of a lunch box. Barry had disconnected a half dozen connection ports.

Smiley came back suddenly, backing up through the door. Sword out.

"Slippery's here and he's not alone."

Down the corridor, Slippery rounded the corner and there were others behind him. He stopped, then stepped aside and the autovolts with him continued past.

Everything was going wrong.

"Barry, you have to go," Kerion said.

"No!"

Smiley told him where to try the voice box and he was angry he hadn't thought of it sooner.

"We'll lead Slippery away," Kerion said.

"Dad, no."

"What would *you* do, son?" He put his uninjured hand to Barry's face, and looked him in the eyes, smirked. "We'll be fine, go." It hurt to lie to the one he loved, but it also felt right. "For your mother and me."

//BULLETSOFLIGHT
SWORDOFGLASS//

"Here they come."

"Well, well," Kerion said when he opened the case.

"What are those?" Smiley asked.

"Cells for the holo-emitters. Which as it happens is very lucky for us."

Kerion took out the raygun and unscrewed the five cells, then threaded five new ones from the foam backing of the case.

"In the corridor, if we can keep them bunched together, or in the doorway this thing will really do the trick."

"Okay, so you do that and I'll do this as they come through. You were in the 7th?"

"Yeah."

"Which side?"

"Does it matter now?"

"Hey."

"Yeah."

"My name is Shohini."

"Kerion."

"It was nice meeting you."

Kerion loaded the charge and lased the lead autovolt. It lit up the head and the robot staggered, misjudging its next step, its chin striking the table, and it moved forward. Shohini swung her glass sword through it as she stepped across the doorway and took position on the other side.

Kerion fired again, he struck the next autovolt in the chest, which scorched and did not pierce, but the second ray staggered it, and as it crossed the threshold, Shohini cleaved off its right leg. The third was calmly trying to step across the difficult terrain of the pieces when Shohini took off its head and closed the door, bracing it with her shoulder. Kerion ran up to the door with her, carrying the case, which spilled charge cells across the floor.

"Reload," Shohini said.

"Reloading," he said, unscrewing each of the charges and tossing them away as he loaded new ones from the floor.

The autovolts on the far side of the door all began to push in unison and the door slowly opened despite all their efforts. Kerion put the barrel against the door and fired. The flash spilled in the room even as it pierced the door.

//JUSTONE//

They withdrew down a winding Funny House corridor of dangling colored streamers and mirrors. Kerion moved ahead, and as he rounded a corner, he nearly walked right into an autovolt standing silently among the ribbons. It turned its head to look at him.

"I am unit 8347-34," Kerion said loudly, hoping Shohini would understand and not turn the corner.

"Incorrect you are a human occupant."

"Exchange to verify," Kerion said.

"Exchange to verify," the autovolt said.

Kerion passed the cable and the autovolt took it, then reached forward with its other hand gripping it tightly. As the automatic man leaned forward through the streamers, Kerion saw the stains of leaked coolant on its shell. Kerion raised the raygun and fired, but it was not fast enough. The two robot hands yanked the cable so hard that the casing, power housing, and clamp ring ripped free with a shower of sparks even as Kerion was dragged forward. Kerion was pulled close and his weapon discharge cut a perfect hole over the autovolt's shoulder through the streamers. A hundred streamer ends fluttered free.

"You are a human occupant," Slippery said.

Shohini swung her glass sword, but again Slippery was too quick and pulled Kerion into the path of the blade.

//STREAMERSANDGLASS//

Shohini diverted the swing, which dug through a mirror into the wall and left a strange negative space of cut-off streamers in its wake. Slippery gripped Kerion by the harness and pushed him like a plow into Shohini, knocking her off her feet. She let go of the sword, which stayed lodged in the wall. As Kerion fell back, Slippery snatched the hammer from Kerion's belt and raised it over Kerion's head with speed and efficiency. As Slippery brought the hammer down quickly though the streamers they snapped taut around it and his arm, tangling.

Kerion pointed the raygun with both hands, trying to bring it to bear from the floor. He fired again and the beam scorched Slippery's shell and the autovolt pivoted and kicked his hands and the weapon. It was like being hit by a baseball bat. The raygun flew free.

Shohini kicked off the wall to get away from them, stood, and went for her sword. She pulled the sword free and lunged, the glass blade passing through Slippery's body with little resistance from back to front. Kerion saw the point leap out of the autovolts body.

Slippery spun, and the force of its body weight against the flat of the blade yanked it free from Shinoni's grasp. Slippery was facing her suddenly and gripped her by the shoulders, then the robot stepped backward, three quick deliberate steps. The hilt of the glass sword struck the wall and thrust the remaining length of the glass through Slippery's back, out his front, and through Shohini's chest.

//THINCLOUDS//

During his run down the corridor and causeway, Kerion had somehow transitioned from the front stage of Funny Landing to backstage. He was in a warehousing space, utilitarian and huge. Metal gantries and stacks of kelpboard boxes. Each box had a barcode that ran round each one like a black ribbon. Light came in from large overhead solar windows.

Slippery was coming around the crates; he must have entered through the hole in the vehicle doors. An autovolt that had survived the raygun barrage was already climbing the gantry to the catwalk. He had a cleaver in his hand. Chop's footfalls rang on the structure. Clang clang clang clang clang clang clang.

Looking down at the damaged housing for his own automatics, Kerion exhaled, a long, controlled breath. He tilted his head and shifted side to side on his feet. He shook out his arms. He couldn't run and he couldn't win.

"Barry!" he called. Loudly and clearly. "Barry, I love you, son. You're going to be okay."

He took out his multi-tool and flipped it open as Chop rounded the gantry on the same level as he was. Kerion dug at his own innards, working quickly, transferring his attention from his task to Chop as the autovolt came forward.

Clang clang clang clang clang clang clang.

PING. A tiny warning chime began to trill in his torso. It was the safety alarm. Kerion had disengaged the safety protocol.

Chop came forward in an even stride and swung his cleaver.

Kerion kicked the autovolt, a straight kick to the leg. A powerful blow with his safety system disengaged which knocked the robot's own leg backward and sent Chop face first into the gantry. The sweep of the cleaver came down on Kieron's leg even as the kick landed. Chop began to get up immediately, Kerion braced himself, holding both rails, weight back on one foot, and kicked Chop as hard as he could in the face.

There was a snap crunch of breaking parts, and Chop fell backward with a CLANG. Kerion's foot was bent sideways off the joint. He hopped backward using the rails for balance, keeping his damaged limb raised as a defense. A warning chimed from Kerion's torso: he had a few seconds, maybe more, before the prosthetics own diagnostics deactivated his legs.

Slippery was somewhere behind him. He could hear the robot's feet on the causeway, a ways away yet, but undoubtedly coming up behind him. Through panels of the warehouse roof, he could see the yellow leaves of the trees against a sun-bright layer of thin clouds. There was hope in all that light.

Kerion had done the best he could. This was it.

Chop's hand gripped the rail and the robot stood straight up. It held up the cleaver again. But Chop waited. There was no reason to wait because it had all the information it needed. It didn't wonder at the strength of the man's limbs, nor the resilience of the leg. It had chosen a new target, likely his heart or brain, and calculated optional means to strike them given the new data.

But Chop waited.

ClangClangClangClangClangClangClangClangClang

Behind Kerion, the sound of an autovolt in full motion.

Then an impact as something hit him from behind and the euphoria of weightlessness as Kerion went over the railing.

//DANGERDUCKS//

Kerion struck the stacked bubble-board boxes of plush
Danger Duck toys, which collapsed under him; the impact
smashed away all his breath. So Kerion lay amid a tangle
of bubble-board and plush toys trying to breathe and
trying to understand what had happened and what he
could make out on the gantry at this angle. A struggle up
there, the whining of servos. Then he saw Chop midair
on its way down to him.

Kerion was scrambling through the boxes, swimming
in the debris of them. Chop landed heavily, punched a hole
in the stack, and disappeared from sight. The whole cube
of boxes suddenly spilled out of its corral, Kerion buried
in that landslide.

Kerion clamored free of the toy pile, dragging himself.
He could hear a sound of creaking, breaking metal above.
He could see Chop, who still had that cleaver, striding
forward through the bubble-board boxes and toys, its gait
switched to low stride, feet barely off the ground as if it

was trudging through deep snow. It pushed the boxes and toys before it and left behind a bizarre wake of Danger Ducks staring blankly.

Then this thing happened. It reminded Kerion of the first time he had seen an autovolt. A way that at once he knew how the world was, and then something impossible broke through and froze him.

The thing was that a cartoon Mega Mouse had leapt down off the catwalk and speared the autovolt through the head and into the torso with what seemed to be a crude spear fashioned from the metal railing. Mega Mouse was crouched on the autovolt, who was still upright, a foot on its shoulder and foot on its chest and grinding the metal spear, back and forth like pulling on a lever, while sparks and smoke swirled in the autovolt's body cavity and chunks of its automatics flew out amid the dull smiles of the piled-up plush bodies of Danger Ducks all around it.

As Chop fell, Mega Mouse let go of the spear and leaped backward casually, landing easily on its cartoon feet in yellow boots between Kerion and the heavily damaged autovolt, yellow cape fluttering as he did so.

Then Mega Mouse turned, and the world righted itself.

The Mega Mouse's cartoon face had been torn away in the struggle, and the smooth see-through surface of its automatic chassis allowed Kerion to see directly into its robot head.

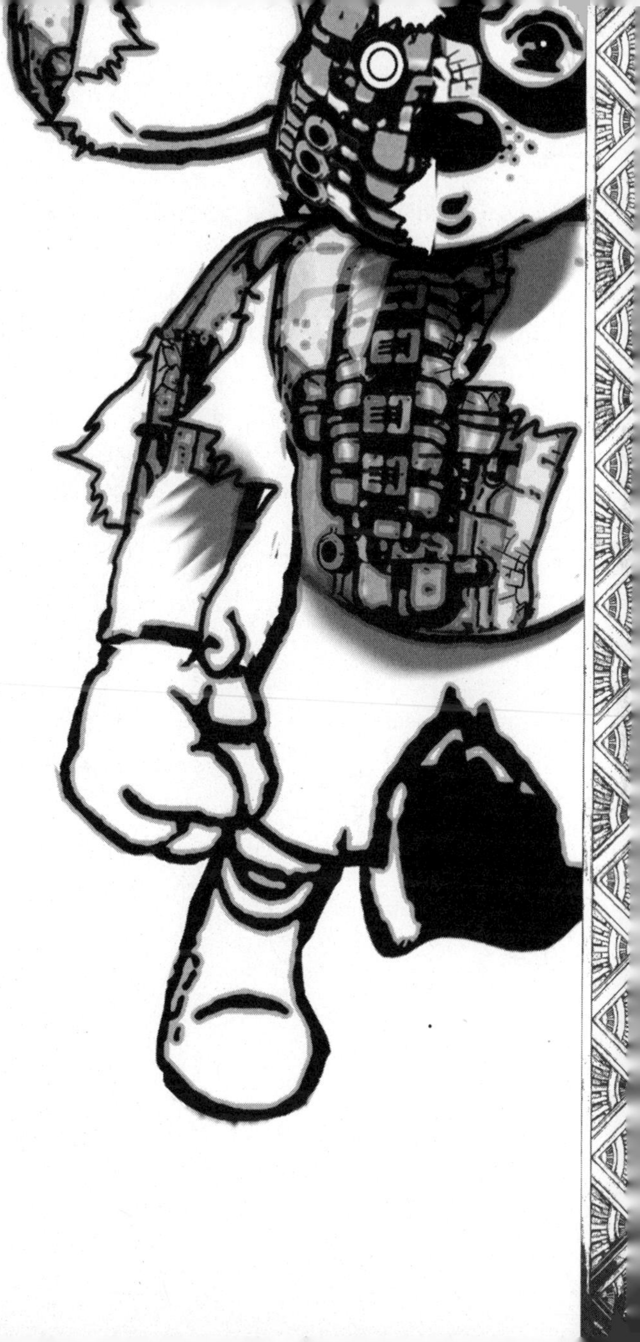

"Dad!" Barry called, panic in his voice, but also that warble of fear and relief.

Barry ran to his side. But Kerion used a sweeping arm to put the child behind him.

"No, Dad, it's okay." Then to the Mouse, "Help me with him."

"Good idea, Bartholomew," the Mouse said in that squeaky cartoon voice as it came over. "Slippery is around here somewhere."

//CARTOONEYE//

"We must go, Bartholomew," Mega Mouse said. Its remaining cartoon eye was huge, its brow furled.

"You look worried," Kerion said.

"It's my protocol to keep my activator safe and do his bidding so long as it does not violate primary protocol," said Mega Mouse. "The autovolts will catch up to us soon if we do not hurry. I can defeat one or two before they overwhelm us, but I prefer to escape."

"Mega Mouse was a security automatic in a fancy toy shell. Smiley figured that Funny Landing's most important person would have its best security automatic. She was right," Barry said.

"Her name was Shohini."

Barry looked very angry, then very sad, then swallowed hard and went on.

"The carousel launches were scrambled. Each carousel has a serial number and their physical launch order lines up the serial numbers and makes it into the code for launch."

"Once I programmed the *order of launch* correctly it unlocked the upward carousels," Mega Mouse said. "They brought me down with them to unlock the tower, so they could get back up."

"Why didn't Slippery take you from the pilot."

"Its protocol forbids it from touching a maker-cube without authorization."

//IWILLIFIMUST//

The launch carousel lay ahead. It was built of rounded ribs of semi-transparent plastic with a gantry up the center. Barry and the automatic cartoon mouse went first; Kerion, limping, came up behind. He leaned on the rail, breathing hard, sweat beading on his forehead.

"Come on, Dad," Barry said, but the dread had gripped him fully now. "We're leaving." That last part caught in his throat.

"You are," Kerion said. "It's *my job* to keep you safe, that's why you're going with him. Because you can start the elevator, and I can reset the launch code again to stop Slippery from following."

Kerion took Barry's pack, and at the bottom was the white voice cube pressed against his son's book of fairy tales. Kerion took it out.

Kerion met his son's eyes with his own. Barry saw the kindness on his dad's face, and the calm. He didn't have to say anything. They both knew. Kerion took a deep breath, held it, then let it out slowly as he rose from the rail. Kerion stepped forward and pulled Barry close. Kerion's automatics were a mess, a section of his abdominal plate was ruptured where the cable assembly had been pulled through. He was leaking stabilizing fluid, his leg was twisted.

"You're my dad," Barry said.

"Forever," Kerion said.

The embrace was interrupted by a quiet chime.

"I'm low," said Kerion.

"Bartholomew," said the automatic, "I do not want to pull you because you are fragile, but I will if I must. Slippery has already signaled others, I can hear it."

At the bend, Slippery jerked into view. His nervous system was damaged, his casing cracked, the wedge-shaped wound of the glass sword spat sparks, but one foot at a time, Slippery was getting nearer.

Behind him dozens of autovolts followed patiently.

Everything was getting caught in the brief narrowing of the moment. Barry didn't say anything. Kerion did not break his gaze. He kept eye contact with his boy until the doors closed and the unit activated, and Barry rode the Backbone of Night into the stars above.

Barry never saw his dad again, a fate he did not wish for but could not deny was the way of all living things eventually.

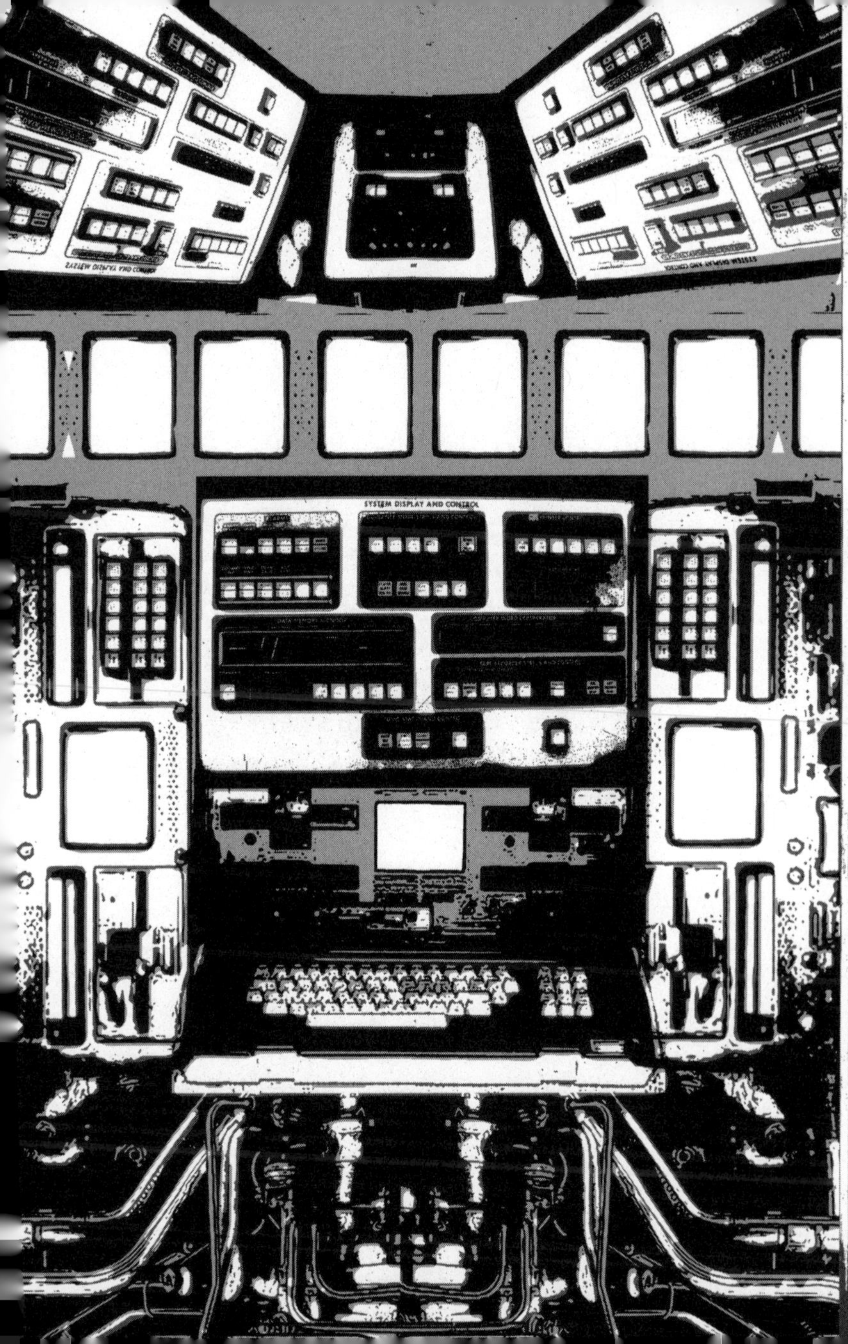
SYSTEM DISPLAY AND CONTROL

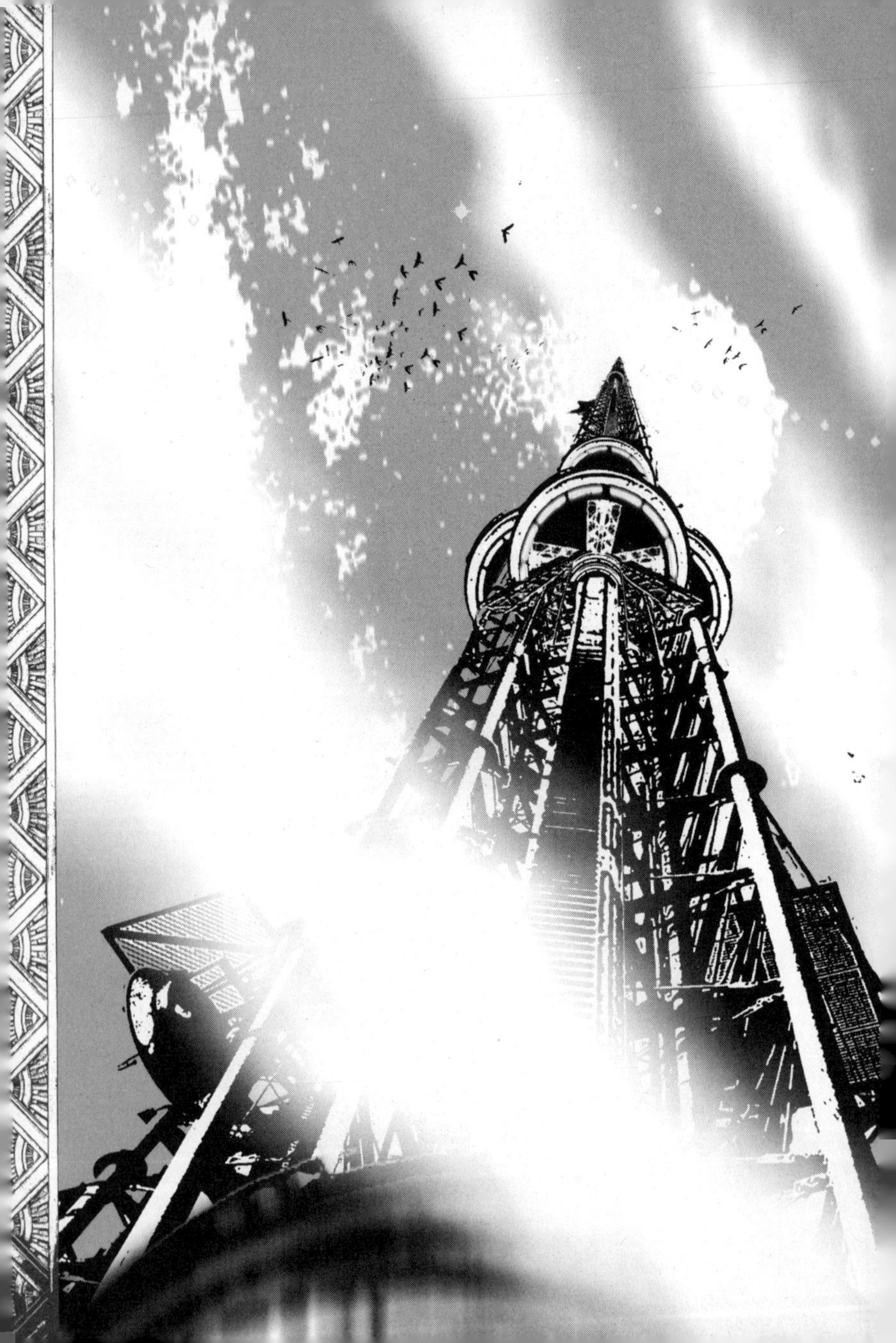

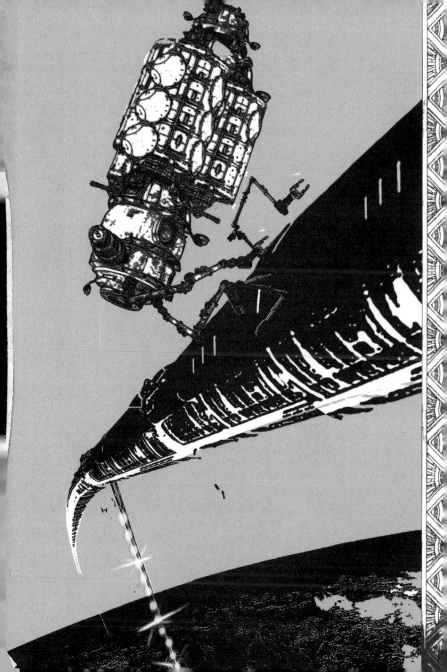

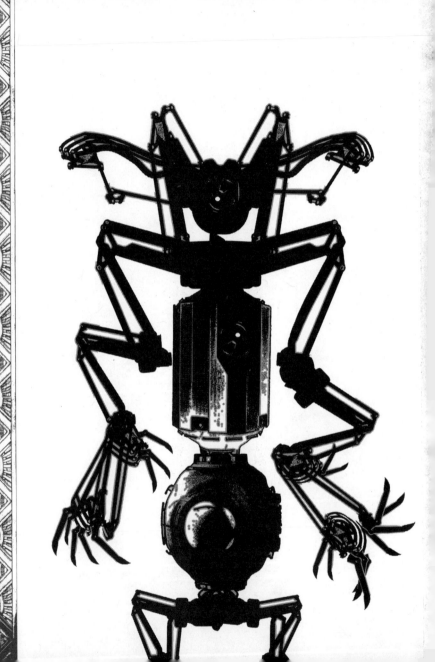